DEATH ON LABOR DAY

BY

CLARICA BURNS

All the characters and events portrayed in this work is fictitious.

All rights reserved.

This book may not be reproduced in whole or in part, by mimeograph or any other means, without permission.

COPYWRIGHT 2021

Printed in the United States of America.

I wish to dedicate this book in memory of my dear sister Emma Lou Mann who gave me invaluable help in all my writing.

If you enjoyed this book you might

Want to try one of Clarica Burns'

Other Novels

Mission of Danger

Mission in Cancun

Mission of Tomorrow

Evil Tribute

Wicked Vows

Capital Intrigue

Mayan Treasure

Red Herring

Hope Eternal

Love Eternal

Death on County Line

When Death Comes Calling

Death Knows No Bounds

And her Young Adult Novel

Winds of Summer

DEATH ON LABOR DAY

PROLOGUE

Mid-summer

Walter Whitney walked briskly out of the prison in Huntsville, Texas. Ten years of his life had been wasted behind those walls, and he couldn't wait to put some space between them. He had lost nearly all his beautiful hair. His hair had always been his pride and joy and now it was all but gone.

He took his handkerchief out of his back pocket and used it to wipe the sweat off of his forehead. He always hated Texas in July and this year was no exception. He stopped and looked around for the cute young thing that had promised to meet him here, and sure enough about halfway down the block was the powder blue Ford Fairlane convertible. Smiling to himself he headed toward it.

The little cutie pie who had befriended him sat in the driver's seat. She had come to the prison with her church group to save the souls of reprobates like him.

Walter had always gone to the church meetings. It had been part of his strategy. He had figured out early what kept the guards and the warden off his back. Going to the church meetings turned out to be one of the main ones.

At the second or third meeting he had attended, he had met Linda Kay. She made him think of a naive child. Her hair, which you could only call mousy-brown, was scraped back in a severe bun. She wore tortoise shell glasses that appeared too large for her face. He had poured on the charm which he had perfected over the years and she started eating out of his hands.

Linda had started bringing him religious tracts on visitation days as an excuse, and then she finally started showing up for no reason. Out of habit, he had continued with the charm, not expecting her to believe all his lies, but she did, and now here she sat in her little convertible expecting him to marry her and settle down.

Talk about naïve, he thought, he had as much intention of settling down and stop his confidence games than he could fly. Walter shook his head in wonderment at the females of the species. He plastered on his serious charming smile as he neared the car.

Linda stuck her head out of the window and waved. Walter waved back and walked a little faster toward the car. He walked up to the window and took her hand and squeezed it.

"Honey Pie, I am so glad to see you without a glass between us," Walter said in his most winsome voice.

Linda giggled and blushed. "Oh, Walter, I am so glad you are finally out of that place at last. Climb in, and I'll take you home. I have a roast ready to pop in the oven and a chocolate cake just waiting to be eaten."

"I can hardly wait," Walter said as he went around to the passenger side and climbed in. He pitched his duffle bag in the back and settled down for the ride.

"Would you like the top down? I know you have been cooped up for so long that I'm sure you would like to have the wind blowing in your face."

Walter looked over at her and shook his head. "That's you all over again, always thinking of others. The top up is okay; I wouldn't want your hair to get mussed."

"You're so sweet," Linda said as she squeezed his leg. Linda pulled smoothly away from the curb and headed away from what had been his home for the last ten years.

"Ah, were you able to get that information I asked you to get?" Walter asked.

Linda glanced over at Walter and back to the road. "Yes, but what you want to know about those men I can't imagine. Your cell mate Kenny, according to my source is headed for Dallas."

"What about Luther Johnson?"

"I wish you wouldn't worry about those men, you should put that life behind you."

"Now you know I have to make sure those two are continuing on the straight and narrow. It's what God would want me to do," Walter said with his tongue in his cheek.

Linda looked over at him and gave him an understanding smile. "Oh, there you go again, always thinking of others."

Walter wanted to laugh in her face. The only reason he didn't was because he wanted the information she had and if she thought he had an ulterior motive she would stop helping him. Actually the only reason he wanted find where Kenny and Luther had gone to was to reassure himself that Kenny did what he had paid him to do. He normally wouldn't ask a junky to kill someone, but beggars couldn't be choosers, and Kenny had been the only one he had available. "So, you're telling me Kenny headed to Dallas?"

"Yes, Mel at the bus station said that he bought a ticket to Dallas. He told Mel he had a sister there."

Walter gave a short laugh. "More than likely, his pusher is there."

"Oh, surely not!" Linda said as she made a turn.

"Honey, once a junkie always a junkie, heroin is a hard taskmaster."

"That's so sad, and I had such hopes for him."

"What about Luther? Did he go to Dallas too?" Walter asked ignoring her last remark.

"Mel wasn't on duty when he left, but he is trying to find out for me. Why do you want to know about these men? I know you think you can keep up with them, but do you think you really should?"

"I owe Luther, and I can't pay him back if I don't know where he is." Walter laughed to himself, he owed him alright; Luther had been the reason he had spent ten years in the slammer; so paying him back wasn't giving him a twenty and wishing him well.

"You are so very sweet."

Walter looked over at Linda and silently rolled his eyes. Did she really believe all the dribble she said, he wondered. Surely, even as naïve as she appeared to be, she couldn't believe he was perfect. He supposed that if he had any good left in him he would leave her as soon as he got his bearings.

"I spoke with Pastor Joe last night and he said as soon as we got the blood tests and marriage license he could marry us. I'm so excited."

Walter looked over at Linda and swallowed hard. "Blood tests, license…"

"Silly, of course we have to have blood tests and a license. We can't get married without them. I thought about going ahead and getting mine, but then I realized I would have to take you to get yours so there was no point."

"Uh—Linda, I think we need to wait a little while. You know, I'm just out of the slammer and—"

"You are so sweet to be thinking about what people will think, but if I don't care, why should you?"

"What about your aunt that raised you?" Walter asked grasping for straws.

"I don't live with Aunt Ellen anymore so she has no say in what I do. Now you just stop worrying, hear me."

"Uh—uh, sure I won't worry about you anymore." He would have to leave tonight after she went to sleep. There was no getting around it. Walter turned his head and stared unseeing at the older clapboard houses that lined the street. He started listing all the things he would need.

The first thing, he would have to use her car to get to the bus station, and then he would need to buy a ticket to Dallas. He could get lost in Dallas; the thing was he wished he knew where Luther had gone. Walter decided he would call the bus station when they got to Linda's house and then he would know more. That decision made, he looked up to see Linda slow the car and turn into a driveway.

"We're home," Linda said with a smile.

Walter took in the white clapboard house with flowers blooming in the flower beds and a large sign flapping in the light breeze that read "Welcome home, Walter."

He looked over at Linda a stunned look on his face. No one had ever welcomed him home before, no one at all. In that instant he wanted to hug her and promise her the moon. Linda's face turned bright red and she giggled nervously.

"I wanted you to know you're welcomed. You will always have a home with me," Linda said as she briskly got out of the car and leaned down to look at a stunned Walter. "Don't just sit there, let's go in the house."

Walter got out and automatically reached in the back for his duffle. "I wish you hadn't," Walter said indicating the sign.

"Do you think I'm ashamed of loving you?"

"No not that, but…"

Linda slipped her arm through his arm and they proceeded up the short walk to the front door. "You don't have to be ashamed anymore. I will always stand beside you."

Walter silently shook his head as he followed her into the house. The telephone was ringing as they opened the door. She hurried over to answer it.

"Hello, oh hello, Mel, have you got any information for me?" Linda turned to the table and began to write. "Yes, I got that. Thanks." She hung up the receiver and turned back to Walter. "That was Mel, he found out where Luther went."

"Where?" Walter asked.

Linda picked up the piece of paper she had written on. "A place called Weatherford. Do you know where that is?"

"Not exactly, but I should have thought of that. He talked about it a lot. That is where his ex-wife lives. I'm not sure she will be glad to see him; I understand from him that their parting wasn't pleasant. Well, well, I will have to get a hold of Kenny and let him know."

"I still don't understand why this is so important, I wish you would just forget about both men," Linda said with a worried frown on her face.

"Old business, honey, you wouldn't understand and I can't explain it to you. If I can't get in touch with Kenny, I'll have to go to Dallas and try to find him."

"But Dallas is such a large place," Linda said.

"Yeah, I may have to go on to Weatherford and find Luther myself. I'll see after I have thought about it for a while." Luther turned toward Linda and gave her a big smile. "In the meantime, didn't you say something about a roast? I haven't had a home cooked meal in ten years, maybe longer."

"Oh, of course, I'll get right on it after I show you to your room," Linda said with a smile.

Chapter 1

Two Months Later

The black 1958 Cadillac Fleetwood cruised slowly around the east side of Weatherford Lake. It would slow almost to a stop and then it would move on. The night hadn't given away to the early morning sun yet; so the headlights of the car pierced the blackness of the night for short periods. In the east, the sky was beginning to brighten just a little letting a person know that the day would be coming soon.

Finally the automobile slowed to a stop. Two men jumped out of the vehicle and opened the trunk of the big car. They reached into the recess and pulled out what looked like a bundle of old blankets. With a man on each end they heaved the bundle out and started silently tramping through the dew laden dead grass. They disappeared around a bend where they were out of sight of the road. They pitched the bundle down and walked briskly back to the car. After the men got back in the vehicle it roared off into the night, leaving its gristly present behind for someone to find.

A bright sparkling September day greeted Roberta Hamilton as she prepared her share of a picnic lunch for her and her three friends. The weatherman had promised temps in the nineties with no hint of fall. Roberta had her ash blonde hair up in a pony-tail and so far no wisps of hair had escaped to wave in the air. This would be the last time for a while that the four of them would be together. Janice, her best friend would be heading to North Texas State University the next day, Carl, Janice's boyfriend would be attending Tarleton State College in Stephenville, and it was true that Eddy would be at Weatherford Junior College with her, but she wasn't sure she wanted to continue dating him. Eddy had become boring; Roberta chewed on a piece of hair while she thought. He hadn't sympathized with her about all that had happened to her three sisters. He told her what happened to her sisters could have been avoided if they had just ignored the problems. She wasn't sure how you could ignore a dead body or someone trying to kill you, and Eddy hadn't known either. She hadn't wanted to argue with him, so she hadn't, but it had left a rift between them. Thinking about it, she wasn't sure she wanted to mend it. Oh well, she thought, that worry was for another day.

When Janice got to the house they combined their food; making sure there would be enough for the guys and of course for them as well. Roberta grabbed a tablecloth at the last minute, after Janice told her that her dad had moved a picnic table onto the lake lot. It would be the greatest Labor Day ever, Roberta thought.

"I think it's really great that we will have an actual table to eat on for our picnic. I really wasn't looking forward to sitting on the ground, no matter how romantic it looks in pictures," Roberta said.

Janice pushed a piece of her white-streaked black hair back in place as she looked into the box full of food. "I know, when Mom told me they were thinking about buying a picnic table I was afraid they meant for next year."

"We could have made do, but I'm glad they went ahead with it this year. Are you ready for college?"

"Yes, I'm all packed and Dad is driving me up tomorrow to check into my dorm. We moved most of my things into the room over the weekend. I am going to miss you." She leaned against the table and brushed a tear away from her eye.

"I'm going to miss you, too," Roberta said as she turned her head so Janice wouldn't see the tears that had welled up in her eyes. She and Janice had been in school together since first grade, how would she go on without her? Janice was taking the parting hard; she couldn't blame her because she was also. It really didn't bear thinking about, and she tried not to. Roberta knew this was part of growing up; the parting from lifelong friends, and making new ones. That knowledge didn't make it any easier as far as Roberta could tell.

"At least Eddy will be at college with you, unlike Carl and me. I am going to miss you all so much. If it wasn't for the full scholarship to North Texas I would just go here to Weatherford," Janice said.

"You couldn't miss this chance and we'll both make new friends, I guess," Roberta said quietly.

"We'll still be besties won't we?" Janice asked almost in a whisper.

"Besties forever, let's talk about something else before you have me crying," Roberta said as she wiped her eyes.

Roberta wiped her eyes one last time as the doorbell interrupted their conversation. She hurried to answer it because Patricia Ann had just erupted out of the hallway. Roberta swung open the door and stopped short. "Hi, Stanley, I thought you were Carl and Eddy."

"Sorry to disappoint you, hi Pat, are you ready?" Stanley asked looking over Roberta's shoulder.

"Yes, I just need to grab my purse," Patricia Ann said.

"You can come in to wait if you like," Roberta said as she stepped to one side.

"Thanks-thought maybe you wouldn't let me in since I failed to be who you were expecting."

"Oh, silly, I really shouldn't have to stand on ceremony with you since you will be part of the family in December," Roberta said teasingly.

"Does that mean I can just walk in without knocking?" Stanley asked.

"Don't be ridiculous, not until after you and Patricia Ann get married."

"I was afraid of that." Stanley grinned as he closed the door.

It didn't take Patricia Ann long to get her purse. "I'm ready, let's go,"

Sarah Hamilton walked into the room as Stanley and Patricia Ann were leaving. Roberta and Patricia Ann's mom was a nice looking forty-six year old with dark brown hair that had gray streaks beginning to show. Even after thirty years of marriage she looked like a thirty year old. Her dark brown eyes were sparkling as she walked over to Stanley and gave him a motherly peck on the cheek. "You two have a good Labor Day; I know Robert and I plan to."

"You know you and Mr. Hamilton can come over to my parent's house if you want. They did invite you," Stanley said.

"I know, Stanley, but I think I'm going to enjoy having my husband all to myself today."

Patricia Ann kissed her mother cheek, "Oh, Mom, you and Dad won't know what to do with yourselves all day alone."

"You never know, we might." Sarah's smile had a mischievous glint to it causing Patricia Ann to blush.

"Mom!" Patricia Ann grabbed Stanley's hand and all but dragged him out of the door.

Sarah turned to Roberta and Janice who had sat down on the couch. "Are you all meeting the boys at the lake?"

"Carl and Eddy are coming by to pick us up. Carl is borrowing his dad's big Buick because it has plenty of trunk space and he can pull the boat behind it," Roberta said.

"You all be sure and wear life jackets if you go out in the boat," Sarah said worriedly.

"We will, oh I almost forgot, I need to get my hat and we'll be ready," Roberta said as she hurried out of the room. She came back with a big floppy hat and her purse as the doorbell rang. "I'm sure that's the guys, Mom, I'll get it."

Roberta opened the door and smiled at the two young men standing on her parent's front porch. Carl Strong, his brown eyes sparkling, a big smile on his face stood in front of the door with his hand raised to knock again. He stood five feet nine inches tall and you could tell by the wide shoulders and muscled arms that he had played football in high school. His friend, Edward Miller stood beside him and was a complete contrast to his buffed friend. Unlike Carl he had excelled in basketball and hoped to play it at Weatherford Junior College. He stood five foot ten and was slimmer than his friend. Both of the boys had crew cuts and today they were dressed in Bermuda shorts and t-shirts with rubber shower shoes on their feet.

"Come in, if you can get the box on the dining room table, we can be on our way," Roberta said motioning the boys in.

It didn't take the boys long to gather up the box and the four young people were on their way. Once they were in the car, Carl switched on the radio and the four joined in singing along with the music.

Roberta broke in as they headed out toward the Fort Worth Highway. "Don't forget we need to pick up ice. Do we have an ice chest?"

"Don't worry about the ice, Eddy and I picked some up before we picked up you girls; we had to ice down the drinks. We are ready to rock and roll," Carl said.

"What I want to know is what you girls have brought to eat?" Eddy asked. "I'm starved."

"It's a surprise. Don't tell them, Janice, make them wait until we get it all laid out," Roberta said.

The rest of the trip went fast, with singing, laughing and teasing of everyone. Once they got to the lake lot, Carl backed in and stopped just short of the water. Eddy jumped out and started motioning Carl to continue backing the vehicle toward the water. Eddy kicked off his shoes and waded out to unhook the boat from the trailer; pulling the boat to the boat dock, he tied it off. Carl pulled the trailer out of the water and killed the engine.

"Okay, girls let's get everything out of the car and see what we have to drink, I am dry as a bone," Carl said.

Roberta and Janice went over to inspect the picnic table, rolled their eyes as they looked at it. They turned toward each other and wrinkled their nose. "Ugh, that is one dirty table," Roberta said as she turned toward Carl. "You wouldn't happen to have a blanket or something in that trunk? We could put it under the table cloth to keep it from getting so dirty."

Carl bent over the trunk and held up a plastic table cloth. "What do you know, I have a table cloth. I think Mom left this in here from the last time we had a picnic."

"That's great," Janice walked over and took the cloth from Carl. "Your mom is the greatest; this will be perfect to put your mom's tablecloth over," she said to Roberta. "Go ahead and bring the rest of the stuff."

Eddy strolled up and pulled out the drink cooler and a large thermos. We have cokes, and Mom sent water, that is if we have glasses."

"We do," Roberta said. "Why don't you all go do some exploring or something while Janice and I unload everything and get it ready to eat?"

"Eddy, come on to the boat and help me make sure it's ready for us to go riding in when we get through eating."

"Sure, we can go exploring later. I want to see how close we are to that creek that runs into the lake. When I was a kid, Dad used to take us to it when it had water in it and we would fish. Of course we never caught anything, I doubt if there were any fish in it, but it was a lot of fun."

"Dad used to take us to the Brazos to swim and sometimes we would fish. I miss that. Sometimes I think getting older is not all it's cracked up to be," Carl said.

It didn't take the girls long to get everything put out on the table. Roberta looked at all the food and shook her head. "It looks like we are feeding an army. I think we'll have a lot to take home and I'm not sure how good it will be left over."

"I'm not sure we'll have all that much left, just wait and see," Janice said with a smile. She turned toward the boat and yelled. "Hey you two come and get it."

"You don't have to call us twice, I'm starving," Carl said as he jumped onto the boat dock.

"I'm ready too," Eddy said following his friend.

After they were through eating and everything had been put away, Roberta pulled out her beach towel and headed to the boat dock. "I don't know what you all are going to do, but I am so stuffed I'm going to lie down and work on my tan."

"Spoil sports; let's go for a walk. After all that food we need the exercise. We can laze later, you know we have all day," Eddy said. He slipped an arm around Roberta effectively halting her progress.

"Yeah, if Mr. Industrious is going to make me walk to the creek, you two should come too," Carl said.

"What do you think, Janice? Personally I'm all about laying around in my swim suit, but it you want to go with the guys we can," Roberta said.

"We might as well go with them or they'll never let us hear the end of it."

"Hey, don't do us any favors," Eddy said squeezing Roberta's hand.

"We're not," Roberta teased and slapped his arm. "Let's go macho man and find that itty bitty creek we've been hearing about."

The four started down the road singing and laughing as they went. Roberta didn't know how the rest of them felt, but she had a feeling this would be the last of the four of them together like this. She wasn't sure if it was college that would change everything, but she had a feeling something was on the brink of change. Roberta suddenly wanted to stop time, the future was scary. Where would they be this time next year, she wondered? Would the four of them even be friends next year? She wanted to date other men, but she was afraid to let go of what she had. Eddy stopped and jerked her out of her useless thoughts.

"Is that your creek?" Carl asked walking up beside Eddy.

"Yeah, I think so. Man, it's little. I remember it being bigger. How in the world did we ever fish in this?"

Eddy asked staring at the small stream that inched its way to the lake.

"Things look bigger when we're young. I remember the first time Dad took us to the Brazos; I thought it was an ocean."

"Yeah you're probably right. I wonder how far back it goes. I remember it being long, like going on forever."

"I think it's wider than it appears from here," Roberta said. "All that grass growing on the sides of the creek hide its width."

"You're probably right, let's see how far back it goes." Eddy grabbed Roberta's hand and started toward the stream.

"Oh, come on, Eddy I want to get some more of those cookies. Not traipse up and down a dumb creek," Carl said with disgust.

"Come on party pooper, I won't go far. If I remember right there's a fence up there somewhere and we won't be able to go any further." Eddy and Roberta waded through the half dead grass following the bank of the creek.

"I'm not wearing shoes to tramp around in the dead grass and weeds, and neither are you," Carl said backing toward the road. "And besides there may be rattlers in all that grass."

"Suit yourself, Roberta and I are going to look," Eddy said as he headed toward the creek bank.

Carl and Janice watched the two teens disappear around a bend in the creek. Janice tugged at Carl's hand. "Come on," she said. "I'm game if you are."

Carl shrugged. "We might as well. Hey, Eddy wait for us."

A scream broke the still silent air and made Janice and Carl stop in their tracks.

"A snake, I know it's a snake," Janice cried clutching desperately at Carl's hand.

"Eddy, Eddy, what's going on?" Carl called out desperately.

Silence beat on the two teenagers ears. "Oh, Carl, do something," Janice gasped out with tears rolling down her cheeks. "Are they dead do you think?"

"Nah, surly not; you stay here, I'm going to see what's going on."

Eddy came back around the bend his face white as a sheet. Roberta with tears running down her face came right behind him. "Uh, Carl, no-no, you don't want to go any further."

"What, why not?" Carl asked. "What did you find?"

"We-we found what I think is a dead body, and trust me you don't want to go there."

"What do you mean, a dead body? We aren't in a TV show." Carl asked almost in a whisper.

"Yeah, maybe we're not in a TV show, but for all of that I know what we saw, and by the way, there is no need to whisper, he can't hear you," Eddy said. "We should head over to the marina and call the sheriff."

"Oh, shit!" Carl said.

Chapter 2

Roberta stared at her friends registering the reaction on what they had found. She still shook all over, and sobs were slipping out when she least expected. Who would have dumped that poor man out in the weeds like that? She didn't think he had been there long; there were no sign of wild animals having disturbed the body; but the ants—the ants all but covered him. Eddy was shaking as badly as she and he had a hard time steadying his breathing.

"Let's get back to the car," Eddy said heading back to their picnic area; not checking to see if anyone followed him.

"Do we just leave the—the body alone?" Janice asked wringing her hands.

"You can go stay with it if you want to but personally I've seen all I want to see," Eddy said continuing down the road.

"Wait for us," Roberta called as she hurried after Eddy. "Come on you guys. The body isn't going anywhere and I have no intention of staying with it."

Carl and Janice stared at each other for a moment and hurried after Roberta.

"Who was it?" Carl gasped out.

"I have no idea. He's an older man, probably thirty or forty. It's hard to tell; the ants…" Roberta shivered as she thought about the body.

"Oh, Roberta," Janice cried as she hurried up and embraced her friend.

"Let's hurry, Eddy is out pacing us," Carl said.

Eddy stood beat over at the waist trying to get his breath when the trio finally caught up with him.

"Hey, buddy, are you okay?" Carl asked taking a hold of his shoulder.

"Yeah, I guess. I thought I was either going to be sick or pass out there for a minute. You better be glad you all didn't follow us. It was a gruesome sight."

"I take it that it was Roberta that screamed?" Carol asked.

"Yes, and you would have too if you'd been there. We thought someone had just thrown down some old blankets and-and Eddy threw back a corner of it and we saw his head." Roberta shivered again and Janice hugged her once more.

"Can I use your dad's car to drive to the marina and call the sheriff? I think someone ought to."

"Maybe we should all go. I'm not sure I want to wait here; what if the killer comes back?" Janice asked. Janice's face had drained of color, and she looked around as if expecting to see a man with a gun coming toward them.

"He appeared to have been dead a while, although I'm no expert on dead bodies," Eddy said. "But really, Janice, if someone disposed of the corpse, I wouldn't expect them to come back to check on him."

"How do you know, someone could be watching right now?" Janice said as she rubbed her arms.

"My experience with dead bodies is that the killer stays as far away as possible," Roberta said trying to control her shivers.

"What do you mean about your experience? When have you been around a dead body before?" Carl asked.

"Didn't Janice tell you, Patricia Ann and I found one out at the old Vaughn place, and I never saw anyone coming back to make sure the body was still where they had stashed it. " Roberta said rubbing her arms. "I don't know just how, but this seems different; more personal...

Janice eyed Carl with disgust. "I told you about it. You just don't remember, or you weren't listening when I told you."

"I guess not," Carl said shamed-faced.

Eddy interrupted the bickering. "We're wasting time; we should report what we have found to the Sheriff. Are you all coming with me or do I go alone?"

"Here are dad's keys," Carl said pulling the keys out of his pocket. "I am not going to the marina and have to face all those fishermen that hang around there. I'll stay here with the girls. We'll have to stay until the sheriff gets here, because we are the only ones who know where the body is."

"I won't be long," Eddy said taking the car keys and heading toward the car.

The trio watched the big Buick disappear around a bend. Roberta unable to sit still any longer got up and started packing up the food.

"What are you doing?" Carl asked as he grabbed a cookie before she put it in the box.

"You may not believe this, but when law enforcement gets involved it will be the end of our day. There will be questions, and it's never short," Roberta said.

"But we don't know anything," Janice insisted.

"That usually doesn't stop the questions, trust me," Roberta said continuing to load the food box.

Janice got up to help. "What a horrible way to end our last day together. I was looking forward to that boat ride and doing a little swimming. I know that's callus to be thinking that way when a man is lying dead not far away, but we don't know him, and we certainly can't help him."

Roberta pulled up a forced smile. "And he won't care what we think or do."

"I think you are exaggerating," Carl said as he watched the girls put everything away. "When we have shown the sheriff where the body is our part will be over."

Roberta looked over at Carl with a raised eyebrow. "If you believe that I've got the Brooklyn Bridge I will sell you cheap."

"Maybe Carl is right, we don't know anything after all," Janice said folding the towels and laying them in the box.

"Okay, don't believe me," Roberta said sitting down on the picnic bench and folding her hands. "I can't possibly know anything about what will happen. Sheriff Young will just say 'Hi kids, good seeing you. You all can go home now.'"

"It's not that we don't believe you," Janice consoled Roberta. "I think it's more the case that we don't want to believe you."

"Well, I for one don't see any point in the deputy, or whoever comes to question us, make us try to tell him more than we know. We haven't done anything," Carl said. "All you did was find a dead body, and Janice and I never even saw it. We just have your word that there is one there."

"Don't you watch television? It's pretty much the same. Whoever finds the body is in for a lot of questions. I know you didn't literally find the body, but Eddy and I did and we can't leave until they are through questioning us," Roberta pointed out.

Carl looked at Roberta as though he would argue with her, and then closed his mouth. Roberta knew he still didn't believe her, but he looked as if he knew she wouldn't change the way she felt. Janice sat down hard on the bench and looked as if she would burst into tears at any moment.

"What a way to end the summer," Janice said.

Eddy got to the marina in record time; he hadn't pushed the car but a time or two he glanced down and realized he was going way too fast. Luckily there didn't seem to be much traffic on the lake road leading to the marina. He pulled into the parking lot in record time and killed the engine. He sat still for a moment, going over in his mind what he should say to the person who answered his call. Taking a deep breath, he reached down to pull the key out of the ignition and found his hands were shaking so badly it took him a while to free the keys.

Eddy opened the car door and headed toward the marina entrance. He was almost to the building's door when it opened and Henry, his older brother, walked out. When Henry saw Eddy he stopped and waited for Eddy to reach him.

"Well if it isn't my little brother," Henry said with a smile on his face. "Where are Roberta and the rest of your group?"

Eddy eyed his older brother almost in dislike. They had always had an uncertain relationship. Henry had the brains, winning a full scholarship to Baylor University; he never threw it up to Eddy, but it did make Eddy feel inferior. Henry was everything Eddy wasn't, assured, deeply committed to his faith, and good looking in spite of the black framed glasses he favored. The girls all flocked to him; some going so far as calling him on the telephone. One reason Eddy had never stopped dating Roberta was because he had a feeling he wouldn't attract anyone else. Eddy wasn't bad looking, in fact a girl or two had even told him that he made their hearts go pitter-patter.

Henry wore his brown hair in a duck tail and his light blue eyes sparkled behind his glasses. Henry always had a smile on his face, and he seemed not to know any strangers. This was enough to irritate Eddy to no ends. Eddy didn't make friends easily. The contrast between the siblings was non-ending.

"Everyone is back at the lake lot. I came here to use the marina's telephone," Eddy replied tersely.

"Whatever for?" Henry asked in surprise.

"Wouldn't you like to know? Actually it's none of your business," Eddy came back. He moved to one side and reached for the door handle.

"Close it down, little brother, what's going on?" Henry asked. "You look like you've seen a ghost, so don't tell me nothing is going on."

Eddy closed his eyes wishing he could bluff it out, but he knew Henry would keep on until he told him everything, what the heck, he thought. "Not a ghost, a dead body," Eddy said.

"What did you say?" Henry asked in astonishment.

"A dead body, do you want me to draw you a picture? We all went exploring and Roberta and I found a dead body," Eddy explained.

"And you left the girls there?" Henry asked in outrage.

"They aren't with the body. Carl stayed with the girls, and besides the man appears to have been dead for a while. No one is coming back to check on him."

"If you say so, is it anyone we know?"

"I really didn't look that closely. We just hurried to get out of there."

Henry followed Eddy into the marina. Eddy walked up to the counter. "Hey, Mr. Houston, can I use your phone to call the sheriff's office?" Eddy asked the middle-aged man behind the counter.

Mr. Houston turned toward Eddy and squinted. "The Sheriff you say; why would a young kid like you want to call the Sheriff?" Mr. Houston lifted his cap that read 'Gone Fishing' and scratched his bald head.

"There's a problem around on the east side of the lake," Eddy said.

"Humph, you just missed Deputy Fisk. He was here about thirty minutes ago."

"Obviously he isn't here now so can I use your phone?" Eddy persisted.

"It'll cost you, Weatherford's long distance you know, and I don't run a charity here," Mr. Houston said.

Henry pulled out a dollar bill and slapped it on the counter. "Will this be enough?"

"I reckon'," Mr. Houston swept the bill up and sat the phone on the counter. "Make the call short or it will cost you more. You know the sheriff's office phone number?"

"Shoot, no," Eddy said in disgust.

"Figures," Mr. Houston said and pointed to a list of telephone numbers posted on the wall behind him. "It's the top one."

Eddy lifted the receiver and started dialing. "Something's wrong," he said.

"Did you put the one in front of the number?" Henry asked.

"Oh, right," Eddy said as he put his finger on the small knob and released it so he could redial. The ringing got cut off in the middle of the second ring.

"Good afternoon, Sheriff's office. How may I direct your call," the cheerful voice said.

Eddy turned his back on his audience and answered quietly. "Is Sheriff Young there?"

"I'm sorry; he's out of the office at the moment. Can someone else help you?"

"This is Edward Miller, some friends and I are at Lake Weatherford for Labor Day, and-and I found a dead body." Eddy thought the phone had gone dead it got so quiet on the other end. "Hello."

"Yes, yes, I'm here; ah, where on Weatherford Lake?"

"It's hard to describe, if the Sheriff or a Deputy will meet me at the marina I can take them to where I found the body."

"All right, I'll send someone right out."

This time there was no mistaking the click on the other end of the line. Eddy assumed he had just disrupted her day. Eddy hung up and looked at his brother. "She's sending someone out."

"I think I'll drive on around to where you left everyone," Henry said.

"Why do you want to do that?" Eddy asked.

"Just to make sure everyone is okay, and to reassure them that you will be along with law enforcement as soon as they can get here."

Eddy rolled his eyes. "Do you even know where you're going?"

"No, but I'll figured it out; didn't you say there isn't a cabin on the lot?"

"Yeah," Eddy mumbled.

Henry laughed and patted his brother on the back. "Don't worry little brother; I won't hog your glory. You're the one who found the body, not me. I'll see you in a bit."

Eddy watched his brother saunter out of the marina. Why oh why hadn't he been born half as assured as Henry, he wondered, and why did it always appear that Henry could read his mind. He shook his head in disgust. All Henry had to do was take one look at him, and Eddy would tell everything he knew and then some. Sometimes Eddy wished he had been born an only child.

Chapter 3

Henry left his brother and headed to the lake lot where Roberta, Janice and Carl were. He smiled and shook his head. Leave it to Roberta to get involved in a murder investigation. Eddy had told him about how she and Patricia Ann found that dead body a few months ago. What in the world was the little darling thinking this time. He would bet she was turning over in her mind what she needed to do to figure out who had killed that man. With her dad being a private eye and her older sister studying to be one, he knew she would be trying to work on this one.

He didn't remember when he had realized he wanted to date Roberta; maybe when she came over to the house just before she and Eddy had graduated in May. He thought for a moment and decided that had to be the time. She was so cute and bubbly; always laughing and joking around, unlike his sober-sided brother. They were nothing alike, and he couldn't figure out why Roberta still dated him. Henry kept hoping Roberta would break up with Eddy, but so far she hadn't, and now Eddy and Roberta would both be at the same college… Well, he could wait; he didn't dare ask her out while she still dated his brother. He figured even if his brother didn't care, Eddy would get angry and give him and Roberta hell about it.

Henry hadn't gotten far when he spotted a lone figure trudging along the road. He slowed up and stopped along side of the man. Rolling down the window, Henry yelled at the man. "Hey, you need a ride?"

The short young man stopped and turned toward the automobile. "I'm good, oh, hi, Henry. I haven't seen you since graduation. How are things going for you?" the young man asked as he walked slowly up to the car.

"Phillip, good grief, what are you doing out here? It has been a while hasn't it. I have been away at college, how about you?"

"You could say I've been in college too, the college of hard knocks. I think law enforcement's wanted list has my name on it."

"I'm sorry to hear that, but it's a new day, maybe things will begin to look better."

"I wouldn't bet on it," Phillip said as he leaned on the window sill.

"You know we're not eighteen anymore. We have to start thinking about our future."

"You may be right. Stealing hubcaps seemed like fun when I was sixteen or seventeen, but not so much anymore. I can't run as fast as I used to.

"What are you going to do with your college degree?"

Henry stared through the windshield for a moment thinking of his opinions. "I'm not sure. I have a degree in psychology with a minor in religion; so I have a couple of choices. I can either go to graduate school and work toward my PHD, or go to Southwestern Theological Seminary and become a preacher. What do you think?"

"Since I'm not what you would call religious, I'm not qualified to give you advice on becoming a preacher. How long does it take to get a PHD?"

"Forever, best I can tell. Are you telling me that if I become a preacher, you wouldn't come to hear me preach?"

Phillip eyed Henry for a minute. "You know I just might."

Henry laughed and slapped Phillip's arm. "I will take you up on that if I decide to go in that direction. Are you sure you don't need a ride?"

"No, I'm fine, besides you are going the opposite direction than I am. I am supposed to meet someone up here a ways. What's going on with you?"

"My little brother found a dead body and is waiting at the marina for Sheriff Young. I am headed to the lake lot where his girlfriend and a couple of others are waiting."

"A dead body, good grief, is it anyone we might know? It is sure strange and you act like this is something common for your brother to do"

"Haven't a clue who it might be. Eddy told me he didn't recognize the body. Probably some of that crowd in Fort Worth. I guess they got tired of dumping bodies in the Trinity River. Gangsters and mobsters seem to thrive in the Fort Worth-Dallas area, I'm glad we're too small a town to attract them."

"You may be right, but sometimes I wish I was living in one of those cities." Phillip looked down at his watch. "I guess I should go on to my meeting. It was nice seeing you."

"Nice seeing you. Take it easy, and if you need any help, financially or otherwise, give me a call. I might not be able to help you, but I might be able to talk you out of what you meant to do."

"I'll remember that offer. I guess I'll see you around." Phillip Johnson lifted a hand in farewell and headed on down the road.

Henry peered in his rearview mirror watching Phillip walk down the road, and wondered about the bad boy persona that Phillip tried so hard to impress people with. Maybe it was his short stature, being only around five-five could give a man a complex. He wore his back hair longer than most men and even had it pulled back and fastened at his neck with a leather strap. He wondered if Phillip really enjoyed the crazy things he did. It was rumored among their classmates that his dad was doing time, and that was the reason Mrs. Johnson had divorced him. Henry shook his head at the strange state of affairs in some families. He was even more determined to go to Seminary in Fort Worth. He wanted the tools to help people like that. As Henry put the car in gear and headed slowly down the road, he wondered if he could help people like Phillip and his mom, or if they would even allow someone to help them. Henry shrugged his shoulders and decided that was a worry for another day.

    It didn't take him long to find the lake lot he had been seeking. He saw the three friends sitting dejectedly on the picnic bench. Pulling into the lot, Henry turned off the ignition and got out of the car. Roberta ran up to him and took his hand.

    "Henry, where did you come from?" Roberta asked. "You're just the person we need. Eddy and I found this dead body, and Eddy has gone off to who knows where to call the Sheriff. It seems as though he has been gone forever."

    "I know all about it; I met him at the marina. Law enforcement is on the way. That is one reason I'm here; I came to reassure you. Hey, Carl how come you let my little brother find a dead body?"

"It wasn't my idea," Carl said as he got up to shake Henry's hand. "I tried to talk him out of exploring, but would he listen, oh no. We had gone down to the creek where your dad used to take you all fishing, and he and Roberta decided to walk along it for a bit. They found the body wrapped up in an old blanket or something; scared the 'you know what' out of us."

"Oh well, Sheriff Young will sort everything out," Henry said. "Eddy has always been inquisitive, but it would have been better for everyone if he hadn't been this time. How is everyone holding up?" Henry looked straight at Roberta, catching her eyes and smiling.

"It is not as bad as when Patricia Ann and I found that body in the old Vaughn house. I wasn't prepared this time. Eddy just threw back the corner of the blanket and voila, there he was. What really freaked me out besides the suddenness of it; was the ants all over him. It gave me the creeps," Roberta said with a shy smile on her face.

"At least now we know why Eddy hasn't returned," Janice said.

"I told him I would come back and reassure all of you." Henry sat down beside Roberta and took her hand. He knew he shouldn't but he couldn't help himself. Roberta looked down at their hands and back up meeting Henry's eyes and smiling.

"Do you think it will be long? I for one would like to go swimming or something," Carl said. "I know that sounds heartless, but after all we don't know the guy so it shouldn't disrupt our day."

"I don't think Sheriff Young would object if you went swimming. I wouldn't think anyone will be here for at least thirty minutes. As I understand it, no one was at the sheriff's office when Eddy called; so they will have to be found and sent out here. Mr. Houston said Deputy Fisk had been at the marina about thirty minutes or so ago, so no telling where he is now."

"I just wish they would hurry, this has messed up all our plans," Janice said with a tear in her voice. "I was so looking forward to spending a carefree day with my friends, possibly for the last time."

"Ah, Janice, don't cry, we will be getting together at Christmas break, you'll see," Carl reassured her.

"It won't be the same, we'll be college kids then and we will have made new friends and—and everything." Janice got up and walked hurriedly toward the boat dock.

Roberta pulled her hand from Henry's warm comforting clasp and hurried after Janice. Henry turned toward Carl and shrugged.

"Women, you gotta love them," Henry said with a smile. "Are you looking forward to college?"

"In a way; I'm going to Tarleton, and no one else that I am friends with will be there. So it is kind of scary."

"I wondered why you were going there, Eddy never said."

"Why else, I got a scholarship. Not a full one like you did, but one that pays my tuition and I'll have a dorm to live in with the rest of the football team."

"You'll make friends, especially if you are living in the dorm with the rest of the team."

"Yeah, but I will be the newbie; that's never good."

"Okay, you're right about that," Henry said with a laugh.

"You have to understand, I am thankful for the scholarship, otherwise I probably couldn't even go to college right now. My folks aren't exactly rich, you know, but I hate not seeing my friends. Friends are important."

"Friends are important, but as we get older you'll find that new friends are important also."

"Yeah, I hear what you're saying, but what about girlfriends?"

"If you really care about Janice and she cares for you, it'll withstand separation."

Carl laughed slightly. "That's just the thing, I feel like I'm using going off to Tarleton as an excuse to stop seeing Janice. I'm too much of a chicken to tell her outright that I want to explore new friends, especially new female friends."

"Oh boy, you have really put a guilt trip on yourself. Have you thought about talking it out with Janice?"

"Are you kidding? Did you see the way she reacted just now to a break up of our plans for the day? She doesn't like change, and we had a fight last night because she wanted me to promise not to date anyone that I meet in Tarleton. I'm not going to promise that. I tried to explain to her that we should explore new avenues of friendship and—you know, see what other fish are in the sea. She didn't go for it."

"I don't know what to tell you, I have never dated anyone exclusively so I can't relate." Henry looked up toward the road. "Looks like Eddy is headed back, so we can assume the sheriff or sheriff's deputy if close behind him. It didn't take anywhere near as long as I thought it would."

Henry watched Eddy pull into the lake lot, followed by a sheriff's car. Eddy got out of the car and waited for the sheriff's car to stop. Sheriff Young stepped out of his vehicle. Henry got up and walked toward the two men with Carl came right behind him.

"Well, Sheriff Young how are you this beautiful Labor Day?" Henry asked jovially.

Sheriff Young looked up at Henry and frowned. "Henry Miller, I might have known you would be here, especially when I realized it was Edward Miller who called this in. He assured me that this isn't a prank call so I'm hoping that's correct since I had to leave my family's gathering to come out here.

"Where's this body you claim you found?" Sheriff Young asked.

"It's down the road a ways. You know where that creek runs into the lake?" Eddy pointed down the road. "Well, it is up from this road on the east side and around the bend in the creek."

"Don't just stand there, young man, let's get started."

"Do you mind if I trail along?" Henry asked.

"Sure, just as long as you don't doddle." Sheriff Young headed out on the road followed by Eddy and Henry.

"Why are you coming?" Eddy asked indigently.

Henry walked along side Eddy and turned his head to glance at his brother. "Just curious, I'm wondering if it's someone we know."

"I see, well, if you must know I got a pretty good look at the body and I didn't know him."

"Good, but none the less, I would like to see for myself; that is if you don't mind."

Eddy opened his mouth and closed it as Sheriff Young stopped and glared at the two brothers. "Are you two coming or not?"

"Of course we are," Henry said with a smile. "Eddy, why don't you lead the way?"

"It's just up the road a ways; you can see the grassy build-up from here." Eddy pointed to a spot about a hundred yards from where they were standing. They were just out of sight of the lake lot.

"Ah, I see where you are talking about," Sheriff Young said.

The trio continued on down the road until they got to the creek. They stopped and Eddy pointed toward the east side of the road and down the creek.

"The body is up there around the bend in the creek."

"You two wait here and I'll go have a look," Sheriff Young said as he headed toward the bend in the creek. He was back in a short time; looking more serious than Henry had ever seen him.

"Wasn't the body there?" Henry asked.

"Oh, yes, it's there alright, not sure who it is but it is definitely a dead body of a man and he has been shot through the heart. Bad business, I sure am getting tired of all the murders that have been happening in my County."

"So what happens now?" Eddy asked. "I mean are you going to haul us all in for questioning?"

"What are you talking about, boy? Haul you in—did you shoot him? I doubt you could hit the broad side of a barn with a gun. No, I know where all of you live, especially that Hamilton girl; if I have any questions I'll let you know.

"Now I'll go back and call for back up and have someone at the office call Whites Funeral Home for a damn ambulance. If this keeps up, the County is going to have to put the funeral home on retainer. Every time a bill shows up from them the Commissioner's Court gives me the evil eye." Sheriff Young headed back to where he left his vehicle shaking his head in disgust.

    Henry looked over at Eddy and grinned. Eddy rolled his eyes and shook his head as the boys followed Sheriff Young back to where they had parked the cars.

Chapter 4

Roberta sat up in bed and stretched. She looked around her side of the bedroom and smiled. She and Darlene had shared a room all of her life and she had grown used to Darlene's rock and roll posters, especially the ones featuring Elvis Presley. Darlene loved his music; in fact any music with a beat that she could dance to turned her on. What could she say; she loved the modern rock and roll music also, but the music with a little country vibe to it was what she dug most.

Roberta realized her part of the room held a more sober tone. A blue spread covered her bed and her little night stand held a picture of the whole family. She wasn't a big fan of posters so her walls were mostly bare except for a bulletin board with her awards from school pinned to it and her achievements in G. A.'s and Y Teens from church. College would be a whole new experience. She wondered if she would turn into a whole new person. Roberta pulled her legs up, wrapped her arms around them, and rested her chin on her knees. College would start next week and she didn't feel like a different person. She felt the same. Janice was still her best friend, she still loved her church; especially her Sunday school class, and she wrinkled her nose; she was still dating the same old boy.

Shaking her head to clear her thoughts, Roberta wondered about the poor man that they had found yesterday. Who was he and who had murdered him? Did his family know he was missing? Did he even have a family? Thinking back to everything her sisters had encountered this summer, Roberta had come to realize that there were really bad people in this world. Her mom and dad had pretty well protected her and her sisters from things her dad had encountered in his job. Maybe that was a good thing, but then again maybe they shouldn't have. Sure she watched Dragnet and other crime shows on TV but those things happened on TV not in real life.

Roberta wondered if Kathleen would help her investigate this murder. She would ask her when she got to work. She would miss going into her dad's office and working. Working part time wouldn't be the same. As her grandpa would say 'she had taken to it like a duck to water'. College was important and if she wanted to be a journalist she would need a degree.

Roberta sighed; she wondered what she was going to do about Eddy. He had been her boyfriend since forever, and he would still be at school with her, but did she still want to date him. Henry, Eddy's big brother, popped into her mind. A smile slowly curled her lips upward. He had felt like a safe harbor yesterday when he showed up. Of course he was older than her; what was she thinking, she never dated older men. She couldn't call him a boy; nope he was definitely a man. Already out of college and ready to take on the world.

Well, that decision and several others would have to wait for another day, because if she didn't want to be late to work she would have to get a move on, she thought as she got out of bed and grabbed her housecoat and headed to the bathroom.

Later at the office Roberta went about her normal routine, making coffee, opening the mail, and sorting through it. Kathleen had a research job at the County Clerk's office this morning and her father had an appointment with the District Attorney so she had the place to herself. She hummed a little as she sorted the mail. She looked up as the door opened and Kathleen walked in.

"Hi, is there anything important in the mail?" Kathleen asked.

"Not really, were you able to find what you needed at the Clerk's office?"

"I think so; I'll run it by Dad when he gets here."

"You got a minute?" Roberta asked a frown on her face.

"Sure, what's up?"

"I wondered if you would help me look into that murder."

"What murder? Oh, you mean the dead guy that you all found yesterday."

"Yes, I know that the Sheriff will be working on it, but it just seems strange that someone would dump him out in the pasture like that. It was like he was garbage and someone had just thrown him out."

"You have to realize people are bad, that goes all the way back to Adam's time. Murder was the first sin outside of the Garden, you know."

"I know, but to kill someone and then just throw him away like that. It seems wrong somehow."

"It is wrong, from the murder to getting rid of the body. Sheriff Young will catch whoever did it. You don't have to worry about it."

"I feel like I am supposed to. It's been weighing on my mind since yesterday. Eddy thinks I'm crazy and won't even talk about helping me. He claims I'm trying to be like you and our sisters. I'm not, not really."

"I know you're not, but trust me, Dad will have a cow and so will Mom if they find out you are sticking your nose into this case. There really isn't much you can do since you have no idea who the victim is."

"Yeah, I kind of wondered about that. Maybe he had a driver's license on him and that will give Sheriff Young something to go on. I still wish there was something I could do to help."

"Why don't you take me through what all happened yesterday? I know the four of you were headed out to Weatherford Lake for a picnic, how did you end up finding this guy?"

"Are you really interested?" Roberta asked. "You're not just Humoring your little sister are you?"

"I'm interested, so give me the details," Kathleen said.

"Okay, here goes," Roberta said and continued to tell Kathleen everything that happened the day before. "That's about it. The sheriff came and ran a few questions past us and they took the body away."

"And you're left with the residue," Kathleen rubbed her arms up and down to suppress the goose bumps. "I hope I never have to see a dead body again. I'm happy checking out insurance fraud."

"Well, what do you think about everything?" Roberta asked.

"Think about what?" Robert Hamilton asked as he came through the door.

"Hi, Dad, Roberta was telling me about yesterday."

Robert stopped and stared at his two girls, a frown marred his face. "No! Understand this you two, neither one of you are getting involved in this murder investigation."

"But just think, if I get involved in this one, you won't have to worry about me anymore."

"You think that reassures me? Besides you don't always have to do everything your sisters do."

"But Daddy—"

"No 'but Daddy' me, and Kathleen do not abet her in this."

"Yes, sir," Kathleen said with a smile.

The two girls were quiet as they watched Robert walk briskly down the hallway. He turned at the last minute. "Kathleen, did you get that information from the Clerk's office like I asked you to?"

"Yes, sir, I'll bring it right in." Kathleen looked over at her sister and shrugged as she picked up her briefcase and followed her dad into his office.

Roberta took a deep breath and tried to immerse herself in her work. For the first time since she had come to work here she couldn't seem to concentrate. All she could think about was the murder. She shook her head to clear it and went back to sorting the mail.

She had just finished when the door opened and Sheriff Young walked into the office. "Morning, Sheriff. How are you this morning?"

Sheriff Young took off his hat and hit it against his leg. "I've been better. Is your dad in?"

"Yes sir, I'll let him know you're here." She picked up the phone and dialed a number. "Mr. Hamilton, Sheriff Young is here to see you.—All right, I'll send him right in." Roberta smiled brightly at the sheriff. "He said you were to go right in."

"You might as well come with me. I don't like to speak to minors unless their parents are there."

Roberta swallowed hard. "Ah, you wish to talk with me?"

"Isn't that what I just said? I don't bite if that's what you're worried about."

"No, I don't think that; I told you everything yesterday so I'm not sure what else you want me to say."

"You never know." He smiled as he waited for her to get out of her chair.

He followed Roberta down the hall into her father's office. She noticed that Kathleen had left and she wasn't sure she liked that.

"Robert, sorry to bother you, but I felt I should stop by and get your take on what happened yesterday; especially since your girl was involved," Sheriff Young said as he shook Robert's hand.

"That's all right, Sheriff. Have a seat. I have informed Roberta she is to leave the case in your capable hands."

"I appreciate that. It doesn't look good for a little girl to solve the case when I'm the sheriff."

Robert chuckled. "I know the feeling. Have you identified the victim?"

"Yep, although whoever dumped him took all of his identification off him; according to what I have been able to find out, he was a well known con man by the name of Walter Whitney." Sheriff Young slapped his hat against his leg. "He had served a ten year jail term for murder at Huntsville and he had only been out of jail about a month or two."

"That's kind of unusual isn't it for a con man to murder someone?"

"Don't hear of it often, I'm sure he claimed self-defense, but obviously the jury didn't buy it."

"So what do you want from me?"

"I was wondering if you or Kathleen would look into his background for me. Best I can tell it is shrouded in mystery and I don't have the man power to do the leg work on this. You know how the Commissioner's Court is about extra men."

"Will they okay my bill when this is over?"

"I ran it by the County Judge and he thinks it will be all right. They meet on Friday so I can get the official okay then."

"So it's on the agenda?"

"Yeah, I made sure of that before I came over here."

"All right, I'll have Kathleen see what she can discover about your man. It shouldn't take much time."

"I sure appreciate this." Sheriff Young turned to Roberta. "Young lady, I need you to give me a run down on yesterday."

"All right," Roberta said quietly. She once again went over everything that happened the day before.

"So you and your friend didn't touch anything at the crime scene?"

"No sir, Eddy did pull the blanket back to see what was there and I'm afraid I screamed, but other than that we didn't touch anything else."

"Well, that's all I need to know for now." Sheriff Young got up and put his Stetson back on his head. "I'll let you all get back to work now. I appreciate you agreeing to help me out on this."

"Think nothing of it. I will be billing the County so I'm not doing you a favor."

"Yes, you are. I want you to get paid this time around that's all. You've been involved in three other murders and you never got paid. This time I'm making sure you get some money out of it."

Robert laughed. "Okay, I'll agree with that."

After Sheriff Young left, Roberta turned to her father. "Can I help Kathleen? After all it's my turn."

Robert eyed his youngest daughter warily. "You really want to be involved in all of this?"

"Of course I do. I'll go and tell Kathleen." Roberta started to get up, but stopped when she saw her father raise his hand and shake his head no.

"Wait, I'll call her to come here. We will need a plan, and Kathleen is still too new at investigating for me to allow her to do this without some supervision. She didn't have any last time, and she got herself in big trouble."

It didn't take long for Robert to tell Kathleen to come to his office and even fewer minutes for her to get there. When she opened the door and saw her little sister, she raised her eyebrow but didn't say anything to Roberta.

"What do you need Dad?"

"Have a seat. I had a visit from Sheriff Young just now, and he has asked us to help him run down some information on the latest murder victim. I told him we would. You keep up with your time like for any other client; we will be billing the County for this job."

"Really? Okay, what am I suppose to find out? Does Sheriff Young know who the victim is?"

"The deceased is a man by the name of Walter Whitney; this could be an alias. Sheriff Young said he had just gotten out of Huntsville, so that will be a good place to start. Find out all you can from the warden. You may want to ask if Whitney had any visitors during his stay in the facility."

"I'll get right on it." Kathleen started toward the door.

"And also, against my better judgment, Roberta will be helping you with your investigation," Robert continued with a smile on his face as he looked over at his baby girl.

Roberta jumped up and all but flew over to her dad and hugged him tightly. "Thank you, Daddy. I'll be careful, I promise."

"Just see that you are, and you too Kathleen, I have enough grey hairs without you two adding to them."

"We'll be careful, won't we, Kathleen," Roberta said bubbling over with glee.

"Definitely, it is no fun being on the wrong end of a loaded gun."

The girls headed toward Kathleen's office. Kathleen stopped before they had gone very far. "Roberta, you will need your steno pad and a pencil. I will make the calls and you will keep up with all the information that I am able to gather."

"That sounds like a plan. I won't be but a moment." Roberta hurried to her desk and gathered up the things she would need. "Okay, I'm ready."

"I wonder if you really are," Kathleen smiled as she led the way to her office.

After getting the Huntsville Prison telephone number from information, Kathleen dialed the number and waited for someone to answer. Two rings later a male voice answered the phone.

"Good morning, Warden's office, how may I help you?"

"This is Kathleen Hamilton with Hamilton Investigations in Weatherford, Texas; I would like to speak with the warden if I may."

"Is this concerning one of our prisoners?"

"In a way, it concerns one of your former prisoners."

"Just a moment, please."

Kathleen put her hand over the receiver and did a thumbs-up to Roberta.

"Hello?"

"Hello, am I speaking with the warden?"

"Yes, can you tell me who I am speaking with?"

"This is Kathleen Hamilton with Hamilton Investigations in Weatherford, Texas."

"All right, Miss Hamilton what may I do for you?"

"Sheriff Johnny Young here in Parker County has asked our agency to look into the background of one Walter Whitney. I understand he was just released from your facility."

"Yes, as a matter of fact he left us a couple of months ago. Has he gone back to his old profession?"

"In that regard, I'm not sure, his body turned up at Weatherford Lake yesterday."

"His body, as in dead?"

"Yes, sir, it appears he had been murdered."

"Okay, I sure wouldn't have expected that. His background is running scams, nothing dangerous enough to cause murder. The only reason he was in jail this time was because he had a target that attempted to kill him. Whitney was able to get the gun from him, and then proceeded to kill him. He claimed it was self-defense, but since no one was around when it happened, self-defense couldn't be proven. I understand the jury decided to sentence him to ten years to hopefully rehabilitate him."

"Really, did it work?"

"I thought so. When he came up for parole, he had a church here vouch for him and he had developed a relationship with one of their members. I understood they intended to get married when he got out."

"Wow, can you give me her name. I would like to chat with her and see if she can give me more information."

"I'm not sure if I should. I will give you the name of the pastor of the church group he interacted with. If he is willing, he can give you her name."

"All right, what is his name?"

"Let me see, just a minute, I will need to look it up. Oh, yes here it is, his name is Pastor Joe Hardy, he's with First Baptist here in town."

"Thank you for your help."

"Not at all, and I am sorry to hear about Walter's death."

Kathleen hung up the phone and looked over at her sister. "What do you think?"

"I think you should call this Pastor Hardy."

"I think your right." Kathleen picked up the receiver again and dialed information. After she got the number she wanted, she dialed it and waited patiently while it rang. She was almost ready to hang up when she heard a breathless, "Hello."

"Pastor Hardy, please?

"This is Pastor Hardy, what can I do for you?"

"This is Kathleen Hamilton with Hamilton Investigation, in Weatherford, Texas; I am calling to find out some information from you concerning Walter Whitney."

"Walter, what seems to be the problem?"

"He was murdered here in Parker County and Sheriff Young has asked my agency to find out what we can about him."

"Murdered, oh, my goodness, may God have mercy on his soul. Where is Linda?"

"Who?"

"Linda, his wife."

"He's married? Okay, that is news. The warden didn't know for sure that he had married."

"Yes, I married them not long after he got out of prison. I tried to talk Linda out of it, but she was insistent. The last I spoke with her, they were headed to Dallas for their honeymoon. That was, let me see, about three weeks ago. I haven't heard anything since."

"Can you give me a description of Linda, her last name would be Whitney now, right?"

"Yes, they were married about a month ago. I don't know if a description will help. She is about five-five, light brown hair, grey eyes, oh, and she wears tortoise shell glasses."

"All right, I've got that down. I will pass this on to Sheriff Young. If she shows up in Huntsville again, would you call me? The number here is 594-3527."

"I'll give her home number a call and make sure she isn't home now. She had told me they would only be gone a week. I know she wasn't in town last Sunday, she's our pianist and if she had been back she would have been at church."

"If you get a hold of her, have her give me a call."

"I certainly will. I'm sorry to hear about Walter. I hoped he had straightened his life out."

"I'm sure his wife felt the same way. I just hope she is still alive."

"Don't even say that, I will never forgive myself if she has been killed too."

"After I pass this information on to Sheriff Young, he may call you."

"All right, you can usually reach me at this number."

Kathleen hung up the phone and leaned back in her chair. "It looks as though Sheriff Young may need to look for another body."

Roberta's eyes had grown large and she gulped. "I sure hope you are wrong."

"I do too, I certainly do too."

Chapter 5

When Roberta got back to her desk to type up her notes, the telephone rang. Picking up the receiver, Roberta answered it absently. "Good morning, Hamilton Investigations, Roberta Hamilton speaking, how may I help you?"

"Roberta, this is Eddy. I need to see you. When is your lunch hour?"

"Oh, hi, Eddy. My lunch hour is from one to two. I cover the phones for Dad from twelve to one. What's going on?"

"I don't know about you, but I don't feel safe anymore. I feel like I am being followed and…"

"You're being followed? Come on Eddy, how would anyone know you found that body? And besides all that, why would anyone want to follow you? It's not like you saw the actual crime."

"I tell you, I know I'm being followed. I went to the administration office at the college to check on a couple of things and this blue Studebaker followed me to the college and when I left I looked in my rearview mirror and it was behind me again. If that isn't being followed, I don't know what is," Eddy said indigently.

"That does sound kind of creepy, but it's probably just a coincidence. Calm down and think, how would anyone know you were the one to find that body, and why would they care. Someone was bound to find it sooner or later, especially when the crows and vultures started circling."

"Maybe no one was supposed to find it that soon. How do I know, I just know I don't feel safe."

"Eddy, calm down, no one knows how long the body had been out there. True the birds hadn't started circling, but you know the scavengers hadn't gotten to the body yet." She shivered. "It was just the ants that gave me the shivers."

"That's just it, I got to thinking about it last night and I feel like maybe it hadn't even been out there over night."

"Really, what makes you think that?"

"I don't know, I guess because the body hadn't been disturbed by any wild life."

"Okay, that makes sense. I still can't believe that anyone would be following you around."

"I think they are and I'm going to go to my grandparent's house in Fort Worth until Sheriff Young figures everything out."

"That seems a little drastic. You realize college starts next week. What will you do about that?"

"I don't know, I guess I'll come back then. I just feel so vulnerable right now. Maybe it's all my imagination, but I can't be as blasé about this as you and your family are."

"I won't say we're blasé; it really freaked us out when Darlene found that dead guy in her car, but by now we take it in stride. Dad isn't happy about it, but other than telling me to cool it and leave it alone, he didn't say much."

"Huh, if it had been my daughter, I would have locked her in her room for the duration. You sound like Henry."

"What do you mean?" Roberta asked.

"Henry thinks I am over reacting. He went out to the marina this morning early and started asking around."

"Asking around; does he have a picture of something?"

"Nah, he's asking if any unusual strangers had been seen in the area. I doubt if he gets any results from his questions."

"I wouldn't think so. Good grief, this was a holiday weekend, I would imagine there would have been a lot of strangers at the lake."

"Probably so, I just wanted to tell you that I'm leaving for Fort Worth as soon as I pack. I guess I'll come back in time for the first day of college. Roberta, one other thing I wanted to tell you."

"What?" Roberta heard Eddy take a deep breath.

"Mainly that's why I wanted to see you and not say this over the phone."

"Okay, what do you want to tell me?"

"I think we should stop dating."

The words came out in a rush and Roberta pulled the receiver away from her ear to stare at it for a minute.

"Roberta, are you still there? I know we have dated since tenth grade, but lately I've felt we maybe should start seeing other people. We're getting ready to go to college, and we will change, and everything. Do you understand what I'm saying?" Eddy explained hurriedly.

"You're breaking up with me over the phone?" Roberta felt like a stone had been dropped on her, she couldn't breathe or even think.

"I know, I know, but I'll be out of town for a week and I want this settled before I get back. I'm sorry, I really am. I still like you and all, but I think that's all it is. I just like you, no other stronger feelings."

"Is this because I won't let you do more than kiss me?"

"No, no it's not. I have been thinking about this for a while now, and I feel we will never feel more for each other than mere liking."

Roberta stared into space for a heartbeat. She grinned and shook her head. "All right, Eddy, maybe you're right. I'm trying to understand, but its okay, really it is."

"You aren't mad or anything like that are you?"

"A little hurt that you felt you could do this over the phone, but mad, no, no I'm not."

"Good, we'll still be friends, right."

Roberta took the receiver from her ear again and stared at it. "Oh, yes, right, friends. I'll see you at college. Have a good life."

"Roberta?"

"Goodbye, Eddy, I have to get back to work. See you around; like I said have a good life." Roberta slowly replaced the receiver in the cradle. She sat very still for a few minutes wondering if what she felt was relief or grief. She suddenly knew what she was feeling, she was feeling empty. Eddy had been part of her life for so long, and now he would be gone. It was like when her kitten died, there had been sadness and emptiness; like something was gone that could never go back and be the same. True she had been thinking about telling Eddy that they should date other people, but she thought maybe they would still go out occasionally, obviously not. Shaking her head to clear it, she went back to her typing;

only stopping occasionally to wipe away a stray tear or two.

The door to the office opened just as Roberta was finishing the report for Kathleen. She looked up with a bright smile plastered on her face. "Hel---hello Henry, what are you doing here?"

"Is that the way you treat all of your new clients?" Henry asked with a grin. The grin left his face completely at the sight of Roberta's woe-begotten face. "What's wrong-what's happened?"

"Nothing, why do you ask?" Roberta said with a forced smile.

"I can tell; I know something has happened, what is it?"

"I shouldn't be telling you," Roberta said as she suddenly felt the urge to bawl her eyes out. "Please don't ask."

Henry hurried around the desk and crouched beside Roberta. "Honey, come on tell me what's wrong."

"Eddy—he…"

"What did he do?" Henry put his hand on Roberta's arm. "Did he hurt you?" Henry dragged a handkerchief out of his back pocket and pushed it into her hands.

Roberta raised her face and tried to wipe the tears that didn't want to stop. "He broke up with me." The words came out so low that Henry had to strain to hear them, and the words were ended with a small hic-cup. He couldn't help but smile.

"I'm so sorry," Henry said.

"I don't mind really," Roberta sobbed out, hoping she could convince herself.

Henry's smile grew larger. "Then why are you crying?"

"I don't know. It's just so sad, you know, an era is over; sorta like graduating high school. You look forward to it, you plan what you will do, and then when it actually happens you feel sad and cry."

"Are you saying you were looking forward to not dating Eddy anymore?"

Roberta nodded her head. "I had been intending to tell him I didn't want to date him anymore; well not exclusively. I wanted freedom to date someone else if someone else came along."

"So—there is no one else right now, no one that you want to date."

"No," Roberta said shaking her head. "I guess that's why I'm so upset. I wanted to be the one to tell him first and not until I was ready. Then we found that dead body and my personal life got pushed way back in the background. I know that sounds crazy to think a crime more interesting than my love life."

"Not necessarily, my love life hasn't been very exciting lately, either, and I find a crime or at least this crime more exciting than my love life or lack thereof."

"Do you really?" Roberta lifted her head and smiled through her tears. "Eddy said I was crazy, and he told me he is leaving to go stay with your grandparents in Fort Worth."

"Really, I haven't heard that. I left early this morning to do a little snooping of my own and came by here before I went home. Why is he leaving?"

"He thinks someone is following him around."

"What? Why does he think that?"

Roberta finished wiping her eyes and smiled. "Paranoid huh, he noticed a blue Studebaker followed him to the college and back and it freaked him out."

Henry pushed up and leaned against the edge of the desk. "Huh, maybe he should be freaked. So then he came by here to tell you about the tail and then broke up with you?"

"No, actually he called me on the phone to tell me he was leaving town and then broke up with me."

"Let me get this straight, my little brother was so crass as to break up with you on the telephone?" Henry asked in surprise.

"Pretty much," Roberta said.

"Boy, way not cool. I think I should apologize on his behalf."

"Don't you dare, it wasn't your fault. In fact, it may have been the best way. It shocked me so much that if he had been here I probably would have made a fool of myself, and it might have caused him to change his mind."

"There is that."

"So, changing the subject, you went snooping, where?" Roberta finished wiping her face and leaned back in her chair.

"I went to the marina and asked a few questions. Not that I found out anything. One fisherman that I hadn't seen before claimed he may have seen someone from out of town hanging around the marina this past week."

"Did you verify that with Mr. Houston?"

"Yeah, and Mr. Houston claimed there were so many newbie's, as he called them, around this holiday weekend that he wasn't sure. I thought I might go over to the sheriff's office and offer to ask around, but I think I need a photograph of the dead guy in order to be of much help."

"Sheriff Young has asked us to help him, and Dad has turned it over to Kathleen. Maybe we can get her to ask Sheriff Young for a photograph. This is kind of exciting; I know Kathleen will do that for us."

"What's this us stuff?"

"Oh, I intend to be with you on this."

"What about your job?"

"Dad may pitch a fit, but he did tell Kathleen that it was all right for me to help her." Roberta smiled a mischievous smile.

"I got a feeling I am going to be in deep do-do with your dad."

"Nah, Dad is the least of our worries. He pretty much doesn't act the heavy father very often."

"If you say so," Henry looked at Roberta and grinned. "So what do we do next?"

"Let's go to Kathleen's office and confer with her." Roberta got up, grabbed her steno pad and pencil, and motioned Henry to follow her. When they got to Kathleen's office door, Roberta tapped lightly on the door and stuck her head around the door. "Can we come in?" Roberta smiled at her sister sitting at her desk engrossed in some paperwork. She had her light brown hair pulled up in a bun today and her glasses securely pushed hard against her face.

Kathleen looked up from a paper she had been reading and smiled. "Have you got that report typed already?"

"Oh, shoot, yes, just a minute and I'll go get it." She turned to Henry. "I'll be right back."

When she got back, Roberta opened the door and ushered Henry into Kathleen's office. "Kathleen, this is Henry Miller, Eddy's older brother."

"Hello, Henry, I think we've met. Didn't you speak at North Side once?"

"Yes, as a matter of fact I did, to your Sunday school class wasn't it?"

"It was. So what brings you here? Don't tell me you need a private eye?"

Henry laughed as he sat down in a chair. "No, thank goodness. I was telling Roberta that I had gone to the marina and asked around about the dead guy; you know, to see if anyone remembered seeing him. But without a picture I didn't get very far."

"That's why we're here, we were wondering if you thought Sheriff Young would give us a picture of the victim?" Roberta jumped in and looked earnestly at her sister as she handed Kathleen the report.

"I don't see why not. Let me call him." Kathleen looked down at the report. "You did make a copy of this I assume."

"Of course, in fact I made two copies."

"Okay. Just a minute let me call the sheriff's office and see if the sheriff is there." Kathleen dialed the number and waited for someone to pick up on the other end.

"Good morning, Sheriff Young's office. How may I help you?"

"Good morning, is Sheriff Young available, this is Kathleen Hamilton."

"Just a moment Miss Hamilton and I'll connect you."

"Sheriff Young here."

"Sheriff, this is Kathleen Hamilton, I found out some things about you murder victim and I have the report ready. I thought if you wouldn't mind I'll send Roberta over with it. Also, she was wondering if you had made a picture of the victim, and if you had, would it be possible for her to have a copy of it."

"I have several copies, why does she want one?"

"She can explain that to you when she gets there."

"Huh, all right. Send her over as soon as possible; you know I never know when I'll be called out."

"I'm aware, she's on her way." Kathleen hung up the receiver and eyed her sister. "Okay, I opened the door for you, but you'll have to convince him to give you one of the photos."

"Thanks bunches, we'll head over there right now." Roberta got up and headed out the door.

"You might want to take a copy of the report you typed up," Kathleen said with a laugh.

Roberta stopped in her tracks and looked at her sister. "Boy I am a dolt. Let's go Henry; we don't want Sheriff Young to bug out on us."

Henry grinned at Kathleen and stood up. "I'll take care of her."

"Make sure you do, she has a tendency to go off half cocked at times, and I don't want Mom and Dad on my back."

"You two, I'm perfectly able to take care of myself," Roberta said with a huff.

"See that you do," Kathleen said as she watched the duo leave her office.

Chapter 6

The TV was blaring loudly as Phillip Johnson strolled into the living room of the small frame house on the outskirts of Weatherford. Phillip ran his hand through his hair and yawned. He reached down and turned the volume down as he headed to the kitchen.

"I'm listening to that," Sophia Johnson said as she walked out of the kitchen with a half smoked cigarette between her fingers and a coffee mug in the other hand. A chenille robe was cinched tightly at her waist and her feet were snug in a pair of dilapidated house shoes.

"Good grief, Phillip, go put some clothes on. It's a good thing your sister has already left for school. You know I don't like you walking around half naked. You may be my grown son, but you still have to follow my rules."

"Don't give me that bull; I've got my jeans on. It's not like I'm out here in my drawers," Phillip said as he frowned at his mother. "Is there any cereal left?'

"I have no idea. You'll have to check and see. If there isn't be sure and put it on the grocery list." Sophia watched her son walk into the kitchen. "Have you found a job yet?"

"Yesterday was a holiday if you remember, so no I haven't gotten one since you asked me last. I'm supposed to talk to Summers Construction today."

"Where were you yesterday then? You were gone most all day. I assumed you were job hunting.

Phillips shrugged as he opened a cabinet door and took down a box of cereal. "I was out for a walk."

"All day, that's no answer," Sophia said as the refrigerator door slammed shut.

Phillip slapped his bowl down on the chrome table and fell down in the chair. "If you must be so nosy, I had a meeting with a guy out at the lake."

"There you go sassing your mother, that's no way to talk to me and as long as you live in my house you will let me know when you go out and where you are going and what you are doing."

Phillip looked over at his mother and grimaced. "Holy cow, I'm twenty-two years old, I'm not a baby."

"You're still my son and you are free-loading off of me, and if you must know, those tips at Jack's Café don't go very far. So as long as you live here you will account for your where-a bouts."

"Okay, okay, if you must know I went to meet Dad."

"You did what? Don't tell me that bastard is in town. I won't have it, you hear, I won't."

"He's in a bind. I just went and talked to him for a little while. You won't let him come here and he knows that."

"Of course, he's in a bind. He's always in a bind. He was running from the law when he left here ten years ago. So do you understand why I don't want him here? I don't want him around your sister and for that matter; I don't want him around you either. He's a bad influence."

"According to him he has spent most of that time in jail, so can't you cut him a little slack."

"I'm sure he has; I divorced him because he was no good, and I didn't want him around us. I have no idea why I was so stupid as to marry him in the first place. He left here when you were ten and your sister barely four, if your grandmother hadn't been alive, I don't know what I would have done."

"If Grandma hadn't been alive, he probably wouldn't have ever left. You know they never got along. He couldn't walk into the same room with her that she didn't jump on him about what a no good he was. You think I don't remember. I remember you two fighting all too well. He couldn't do anything right. He didn't say what he was in jail for, but it probably was because he wanted to make enough money to come back here and show you he wasn't a no-account."

"He left because the Sheriff from Tarrant County was on his tail, so don't give me anymore sass about your grandmother. We wouldn't have a roof over our heads if she hadn't taken us in. If he's back, he wants something. Probably money, he was always short of money."

"You'll be glad to know he doesn't want anything from you; he just wanted to see me."

"I should hope not, and I'll tell you this; if he shows up here I'll get after him with your grandpa's shotgun."

Phillip got up from his chair and put his bowl in the sink, he turned to head out of the kitchen.

"What are you doing? I'm still talking to you," Sophia said as she watched Phillip stalk out of the kitchen.

"I'm tired of hearing you bad mouth my dad, so I'm going to shower and dress, and then I'm going to head into town to see about that job I told you about. Is that okay with you?"

"Humph, I suppose so, but let me tell you that I won't have you seeing your dad anymore, do you hear me?"

"Whatever you say," Phillip mumbled as he headed toward the bathroom.

Sophia watched him leave the kitchen and head down the hallway. She glanced at her watch and frowned. She needed to get dressed or she wouldn't have time to go to the grocery store and get back before her shift at the café started. She smiled to herself, it was Tuesday night and that cute trucker that stopped at Jack's always came in on Tuesday night. She wished she knew more about him. He didn't wear a ring, but that didn't tell her anything. She stubbed out her cigarette, turned the sound back up on the TV and headed to her bedroom.

It didn't take Phillip long to get ready and head out the door for his interview. He had hopes that Summers Construction would hire him. He had spoken with Harold Summers on Friday and he had told him to stop by the office in downtown Weatherford and they would talk. He knew he didn't have a lot of experience in construction, but he also knew he could learn.

When he pulled up in front of the construction company's office, he sat still for a minute and proceeded to give himself a stern talking to. His hands were damp and sweaty and it wasn't from the heat. He really needed this job, and he had promised his dad that he would ask Mr. Summers if he might need another hand. His dad was out of jail, but if he didn't find a job soon Phillip was afraid that his dad would slip back into petty theft which was probably what got him sent to Huntsville.

Phillip walked into the office and a young girl sat at the reception desk. She was a cute little thing, Phillip noted. With her light blond hair and her ruby red lips, but he could also tell she was under-age so not for him. "Hello, may I help you?"

Phillip pulled his baseball cap off of his head and held it in front of him. "Ah-ah, yes, I was hoping to see Mr. Summers about a job. He told me to come in today." Phillip shifted from one foot to the other, the last time he had felt this nervous was when he had been sent to the principal's office at school.

"Just a moment and I'll check. Won't you have a seat," she said as she indicated a wooden chair across from her desk.

Phillip sat down and waited, getting more nervous by the minute. Finally the young lady looked up and smiled. Mr. Summers will see you now."

"Ah, thank you, which way?"

"I'll show you. Are you new in Weatherford?" she asked, her smile almost knocking him down with its brilliance.

"No, I've lived here most of my life. My mom, sister and I live off the Fort Worth Highway."

"Oh, you must be older than I thought, I will graduate this May and I thought I knew everyone in the high school."

"I graduated about four years ago."

"That's the reason I didn't recognize you. Here we are." The young lady tapped lightly on the door; a muffled 'come in' came through the door. She moved to one side. "You can go on in."

Phillip opened the door and squared his shoulders as he walked in. "Mr. Summers, I'm Phillip Johnson; we spoke last Friday."

"Yes, of course, I remember now, come in and have a seat. You're looking for a job I understand."

"Yes, sir, I am. I don't have a great deal of experience but I'm a quick learner." Phillip sat down in a chair that was pushed against the wall. He didn't know if he should have started with the no experience bit, but neither did he want Mr. Summers to expect more than he was able to give.

Harold Summers put his finger tips together and eyed the young man sitting in front of him. He had to be twenty-one or two and he looked to be as nervous as all get out. He had seen men like this before and they usually were men who didn't have much luck getting or retaining a job. Oh well, he thought, since they had opened the new section of updated floor plans and had also acquired the bid on the college he was in desperate need of more construction workers and they had to learn some way.

"Do you own a hammer?" Harold asked as he pushed his hair out of his face.

"No, but I can buy one. Where do I go to buy a good one?"

"Well, don't go to the dime store, I'm not saying their hammers aren't good; it's just that you will want one to last you a while. Go to one of the hardware stores on North Main and tell them you need a hammer for a construction job you are starting tomorrow."

"You mean I'm hired?" Phillip asked his eyes grew round with surprise and excitement.

"I need warm bodies at the construction site we have going on."

"Could you use someone else?"

"You know someone who is looking for a job?"

"Yes, sir, my dad; he, huh," Phillip swallowed hard. "He just got out of Huntsville, not anything major you understand. I think he got hooked up with a con artist and there was a major blow up with one of the marks. He's been out for about a month or two and really could use the work. He's been doing odd jobs for people, but it's not steady and it's not enough to live on." Phillip waited breathlessly as the man across from him stared at him without blinking. He figured he had just blown it and Mr. Summers would tell him not only would he not hire his dad but that he didn't need him after all.

"How old is your father?"

"What? Ah, I'm not sure, in his late forties maybe."

"Okay, tell him to come by and see me, but I'm sure I can use him; if for nothing else he can do clean-up and run odd errands for the crew."

"Oh, thank you, he'll do anything."

"But you tell him the first slip up and he'll be out on his tail. Now you go to the front and fill out your paperwork and I'll see you tomorrow at the job site."

"Yes, sir, I'll be there, and thank you again for taking a chance on my dad."

"You just make sure I'm not sorry for my decision."

"I will, oh, where is the job site?"

"I'm sending you out to where we are building some houses off of Tin Top Road. You do know where that is, don't you?"

"Yes, sir, I'll be there at eight o'clock sharp." Phillip got up and shook Harold's hand.

"See that you are. My brother Barry is the foreman on that site, so just ask for him."

"Yes, sir," Phillip took a deep breath and walked out of the office with a new confidence in his step. He knew his mother would be thrilled and he felt relieved that his father would now not have an excuse to get himself in trouble again.

Henry and Roberta went into Sheriff Young's office and sat down in the chairs in front of his desk. Henry noticed that Sheriff Young's hat was on his desk and he looked at them impatiently. His graying hair was cut close to his head and he leaned back in his chair and touched the tips of his fingers together, looking at them.

"I was on my way out of here when you two showed up. Miss Hamilton asked about a picture of the murder victim. Why do you want it?"

"I fish quite a bit around the marina, and I thought I could show the picture around to see if anyone had seen him there," Henry said. "I did speak with a few of the fishermen this morning and no one had noticed any strangers around."

"You want to be a deputy now?" Sheriff Young asked.

"Not particularly, I just wanted to help, and I thought maybe people might come near talking with me than with law enforcement. Roberta tells me that you have asked her dad's office to help you so I would work under Mr. Hamilton's direction." Henry felt as though his oxford shirt collar that was open at the neck was strangling him.

Sheriff Young's penetrating gaze made Henry feel uncomfortable, and he shifted in his chair. He noticed Roberta was crossing and uncrossing her legs.

"Young man, I don't know who you think you are but I can do my own investigating." Sheriff Young looked over at Roberta. "What about you, are you going to stick your nose into this case?"

"Ah-ah, not if you don't want me to, I have typed up Kathleen's report on her conversation with the warden at Huntsville and she asked me to bring it to you. If you don't want me or Henry to help then we won't."

"Humm, I won't say a little help wouldn't come in handy, but I don't want this spread around. Let me see that report."

Roberta handed the report to the sheriff, sat back and waited for him to read it. Instead he laid it down on his desk and made no attempt to read it. "Give me the highlights," Sheriff Young ordered.

Roberta took a deep breath and began. "The warden told Kathleen that a lady picked up Whitney when he got out. He also gave her the name of the church group that the lady was associated with. Kathleen called and spoke with the pastor of the church; he told her that Whitney and the lady were married. The lady told the pastor that she and Whitney were coming to Dallas for their honeymoon."

"Did she get a name?"

"Yes sir, that's in the report. Also the name and phone number of the pastor. He told Kathleen that if the lady called him, he would let her know."

"I hate to think of some innocent being involved with someone like Whitney." Sheriff Young opened a file folder and pulled out a picture. "Here's Whitney's mug shot when he was arrested. It's pretty close to the way he looked in death. If you run across anyone who remembers seeing him, be sure and get their name and phone number." Sheriff Young handed the photo to Henry and turned to Roberta. "You ask Miss Hamilton if she'll call that pastor back and see if he has a picture of the woman Whitney married. If he has one, ask him to overnight it to me."

"I'll do that. I'm surprised we didn't think of asking about a picture of her. The pastor hoped she was home."

"Not likely, if they were married, she would have stayed with her husband. I'm just hoping we won't find her body somewhere. I'll call Tarrant and Dallas County sheriffs and see if they have any unidentified female bodies, but I'll need her picture."

"We'll get right on that. Thank you; we appreciate you letting us have that picture." Roberta rose from her chair, shook the sheriff's hand and waited while Henry shook the sheriff's hand also.

"Do you think this was a case of wrong time-wrong place?" Roberta asked.

"What I think is Whitney got himself in a bunch of trouble that he wasn't used to and it got him killed. You two be careful, you hear?"

"Oh, we will and we'll keep you informed of what we find out," Roberta said breezily as she led the way out of the door.

Chapter 7

Henry and Roberta got in his car and looked at each other for a few minutes. "Whee!" Henry said with a slight grin on his face. "I don't think the sheriff is too happy with us, do you?"

"Didn't seem like it, but at least we got the picture. Let me see it," Roberta said holding out her hand.

Henry handed it to her. "Do you recognize him?"

"Nope, he doesn't look like a criminal, does he?"

Henry laughed. "What do you think a criminal looks like?"

"Oh, I don't know, you know beady eyes and a scowl on his face, sorta like Edward G. Robinson."

"Honey, that's in the movies, not in real life."

"Maybe," Roberta stopped what she started to say and looked hard at Henry. "What did you call me?"

"Oops, sorry, it slipped out." Henry glanced over at Roberta and started the car. He concentrated on backing out of the parking place and didn't look back at her. He almost blew it. He should watch what he says when she was around or he would scare her away. "Do you want to ride out to the lake with me and check out this picture?"

"Wish I could, but I really need to get back to work. I will only be working part time after college starts next week. I'm sure going to miss going in every day."

"You've really enjoyed working there, haven't you?"

"Sure, I mean, I have the best of both worlds. I get paid and I work with my dad and sister. And it's kind of exciting, you know. Oh, I don't mean that we investigate murders every day. I think that is an anomaly, but just to see how many people think they can get away with lying, cheating and stealing is amazing."

"Some people would say that wouldn't be a good situation, working with your family like that, but I can see where the job might be interesting."

"As long as I do my work, I don't have any problem with Dad, and Kathleen is a breeze to work for. She and I are pretty close, and always have been."

Henry pulled into a parking place in front of the office building and waited until Roberta got out. She leaned down and laid her arms on the window sill of the car. "Let me know what you find out, okay?"

"Sure, I'll give you a call tonight, that is unless I break the case wide open and come hurrying back to brag."

Roberta laughed and shook her head. "Either way it sounds like a winner. Bye." Roberta stood up and waved a hand as Henry started backing out of the parking space.

Henry wasn't happy that Roberta hadn't wanted to come with him, but he could understand that she needed to get back to work. He needed to find a job, too and not just odd jobs for his dad. He really wanted to go to Southwestern Baptist Theological Seminary in Fort Worth, but there again he seemed to be dragging his feet. So much to do and so little time, he thought.

He had slipped up with the 'honey' bit, but at least she hadn't pushed it. He needed to get his mind off Roberta and back to what he would do once he was back at the marina. He glanced over at the file folder the sheriff had put the photo in and couldn't decide on the approach he wanted to use. Some of the guys that were regulars, he could just walk up and ask them if they knew Whitney, but others you would have to handle with kid gloves.

When he pulled up in front of the marina building, he noticed a large black 1958 Cadillac DeVille parked away from the other automobiles. Whimsically, he thought, it was as if the Cadillac had its nose up in the air and felt it was too good for the old beat up pickups and older model cars parked on the lot. He raised an eyebrow as he got out of his little 1950 Chevy. He wondered who it could be. They certainly didn't get many cars of that class here. He sauntered up to the door of the marina just as one of his old fishing buddies came out.

"Hey, Matt what you up to, are you giving up for the day?" Henry asked as he stretched out his hand and shook Matt's.

"Ah, a Miss Highfalutin is in there, ruined the whole atmosphere of the place. Thought I might head into town and grab me a burger at A & W. Maybe by the time I get back she'll be gone and I can get me some more bait." Matt shook Henry's hand and took his straw hat off and slapped it beside his leg. "Can't fish without bait you know and I'm too lazy to dig up worms. Come on with me," he invited.

"I may catch up with you later. I got a picture I want to show you, if you don't mind looking at it."

"Sure, I'm not in any hurry; just had to get out of there." Matt threw his head back to indicate the building behind him. "What you got there a pin up, maybe something out of Playboy?"

"Not hardly; have a look." Henry took the picture out of the file folder he had in his hand and handed it to Matt.

Matt looked quietly at the picture for a minute, set his hat back on his head and frowned at Henry. "Are you associating with known criminals now?"

"No, do you recognize him?"

"I've seen him around," Matt frowned. "About a week ago I think it was. He was asking about Luther."

"Luther-Luther who?"

"Oh, I guess he would have been before your time. Luther Johnson, he married my grandma's best friend's granddaughter. We all kinda grew up together.

Luther, he had an itch, I knew he wouldn't stay around here long; and he didn't. He married Sophia Bernard; course Sophie, she threw him out finally, claimed he was no good and she didn't want him around the kids."

"Is that Phillip Johnson's dad?"

"Was that the boy's name, there's a girl too I think. Sophie's a waitress down at Jacks."

"Did you tell the guy in the picture where to find Luther?"

"Nah, like I say we grew up together, you don't rat out your friends. Besides hadn't seen Luther in a month of Sunday's or longer. You know now that I think about it, ole Blevins might have told this dude something."

"Do you think Mr. Blevins may have seen Luther?"

"Nah, but he likes to seem important, he probably shot him a line of bull about where Luther might be. I know one place Luther wouldn't be, and that is with his ex-wife. She'd just as soon shoot him as look at him. She's one mean ole gal."

"Well, thanks for the information, Matt."

"Can't remember that dude's name, Whitey, Whitley," Matt continued as if Henry hadn't spoken. "You know the funny thing is; Miss Highfalutin in there is asking about Luther also, talk about coincidence."

"She's asking about Luther?"

"Didn't I just say that? Yep, she's standing in the middle of the store with her nose all wrinkled up like she smells something dead and demanded-demanded mind you that if anyone knew the whereabouts of a Mr. Luther Johnson they should come and talk to her, any viable information regarding where he was would earn that person a fifty dollar bill. Some men would kill their mama for a fifty dollar bill, much less rat out a friend."

Henry couldn't help a smile from forming on his lips. "And you're not one of those friends."

"Hell, no, excuse my French. If Luther's got himself in a heap of trouble, he can get out of it without my help."

"Do you think Luther's around here somewhere?"

"Could be he grew up around here, and there are still old barns and tumbled down houses that weren't torn down when the City built this here lake. Why do you ask?" Matt frowned at Henry.

"On Labor Day I ran into Phillip walking around on the east side of the lake. It seemed kind of strange to me."

Matt pursed his lips and nodded. "Could be ole Luther got in touch with his son and the boy went to see him. If I recall there's a half-way decent vacant house not far from that creek that runs into the lake on the east side."

"Shoot!"

"What's wrong?"

"Oh nothing, just thinking, thank you for the information you have given me. I won't go into the marina; I wouldn't want to run into Miss Highfalutin. By the way do you have an actual name for her?"

"I believe she said her name was Jacob," Matt thought for a minute. "That's right she said her name was Lana Jacob I reckon she owns that big Caddy over there. It looks like it thinks it's too good for the likes of my old truck. Well, I'll see you around and if you want to join me at the A and W come on."

"Okay, thanks, I'll probably see you around maybe tomorrow. I'm helping my dad out some and I'm not always able to get out here to fish."

"Too bad about that, my old lady tells me I need to get a steady job, but hey, doing odd jobs for people is as steady as it comes." Matt laughed as he headed toward a beat up 1940 Chevrolet pickup.

Henry shook his head and went back to his car. He wasn't sure what to do with the information Matt had given him, he couldn't decide if he should go straight to Sheriff Young or let Kathleen and Roberta know first. In reality he wasn't sure he even had anything, it wasn't a crime to walk around the lake, but if Phillip had met with his dad and if his dad had known Whitney… As people say, there are no coincidences. He'd decide on the way back into town. His first thought was to take it to Sheriff Young, but if he wasn't in his office it wouldn't do any good to go there first. Besides if he took it to Mr. Hamilton's office he would get to see Roberta and that was definitely a plus. He grinned to himself, Hamilton Investigations it would be. He didn't even have to flip a coin.

As Henry pulled out of the parking lot a smartly dressed woman in her late fifties walked briskly out of the marina. She was tall for a woman, she seemed to be trying hard to reach six foot, but not quite making it. She wore her grey hair in a smooth bun at the base of her neck, this with her severe charcoal grey business suit and black low heel pumps proclaimed her as a no nonsense woman. She glanced at the taillights of Henry's car as he pulled onto the road. She really was pissed that she had not found out anything in that smelly marina. She had been sure one of the drifters and no-goods would have told her something, after all she had offered them fifty bucks to rat out a friend. Those kinds of people in there would usually do about anything for fifty dollars. If Kenny was right and this Luther person would help her out, then it would be worth the fifty dollars to get information on him.

Lana wished she could have used Kenny, but as her mother said he was just too unreliable. How in the world could her mother have married Kenny's father, she would never figure that out. Both of them were no good as far as she was concerned, but Kenny had come in handy by giving her the name of someone who might be willing to kill a couple of men for her. Sometimes a woman who wanted to get ahead had to use all the means available to achieve her ends. She figured that with Mr. Williams and that no good lying piece of shit Anderson were gone, she would be the next CEO of the company. She was back to square one, but Kenny might still have some more information, all she would have to do was hold up Kenny's next fix and he would sing like a bird. A cruel smile broke her face as she walked determinedly to her car.

Chapter 8

Lana pulled into Jack's Café parking lot and sat for a moment going over in her mind what she had learned or rather what she hadn't learned at the marina. She supposed her next item on the agenda would be to call Kenny and see if she could get him to tell her anything more about this Luther Johnson. She had to find him, she just had too. She checked her purse for change and came up with a couple of dollars in quarters. Hopefully that would be enough for the pay phone.

Getting out of her car, Lana walked briskly into the café. She had seen two or three cars pull up while she had been sitting and counting her change, but it was still a little early for lunch so the café wasn't full. Good, she thought, maybe that way she wouldn't be overheard.

Lana stopped a waitress on her way to a table. "Pardon me; do you have a pay phone that I may use?"

The waitress paused for a moment and shrugged, pointing the way, "yeah, over in the hallway toward the bathrooms."

"Thank you," Lana said as she walked sedately toward the short hallway. She looked back to see if anyone was watching and noticed a couple of men giving her the eye. They stood out because unlike the truckers, farmers and ranchers who seemed to make up most of the patrons, these two had on suits and if she wasn't mistaken they were both armed. Lana wondered briefly if they were for sale and if they might be willing to do her job. Maybe she should approach them and ask if they were guns for hire. Shaking her head, she gave a short laugh at her silliness and continued on to the telephone that she had spied hanging on the wall just inside the hallway.

It didn't take long to get Kenny on the phone even if he did sound as if he was high on his drug of choice. "Kenny, listen I need you to give me more information on Luther."

"Oh, hi, sis, what you need? I don't need anything right now; I'm feeling so good," Kenny said in a befuddled way.

"I told you what I want. I need more information. Listen up; give me more information on Luther."

"Luther who?" Kenny asked. "I don't know who you are talking about. I'm flying, did you know that; soaring through the sky like a bird."

Lana rolled her eyes. "Really, Kenny, concentrate, I need more information on Luther Johnson, your ex-cell mate. You said he might be willing to do me a favor for the right amount of money."

"Ah, sis, I just made that up. Ole Luther he ain't no killer. He's just a guy who got tangled up with a con-man, you know. He won't do any killing. I think he's afraid of guns."

"You told me he would; that is why I made this useless trip to Weatherford, so help me are you shooting me a line of bull this time or last?"

"You kept me from my sweetheart; I'd tell you anything to get my sweetheart."

"I'll make sure you never get anymore of your sweetheart if you don't straighten up and tell me what I want to know."

"I told you, Luther ain't no killer. Hell, I'd come near killing someone than he would. You wouldn't really keep my sweetheart from me, would you?"

"Oh, yes I would. Even if you think Luther wouldn't do this for me, I'm going to talk to him if I can find him. Tell me some more about him."

"Ain't much more to tell that I know of, he has an ex-wife in that berg and a couple of kids. He told me he was going to go see the kids. He said his ex would probably shoot him on sight if he showed up at her place. I don't know how he planned to see his kids; he didn't say."

"Where is her place, do you know?"

"Nah, he never said. He weren't much of a talker. He did say he liked to fish, and since there was a new lake there that had been built since he had been home, he wanted to try it out."

"You told me that. I checked at the marina and if anyone had seen him they weren't talking. Probably figured I was with the law. One guy did say he thought he knew where he might be, but he would have to show me, because he couldn't tell me where it was."

"Probably stringing you along, you offered money for information didn't you? I told you not to do that. People will rat out their best friend or family for money."

"I only offered fifty dollars; I wasn't getting anywhere just talking. I had to sweeten the pot."

Lana heard a laugh coming over the line. "Don't laugh at me, I did what I thought best, so don't give me any bull."

"Well, I don't got no more to tell you so you can stop harassing me."

Lana heard a very loud click indicating he had hung up. She rested her head against the wall as she hung up the receiver. She wondered what she was going to do now, but she didn't have an answer.

Lana walked over and sat down at a table, she decided that she might as well eat something before she headed back to Dallas. It had certainly been an unproductive day. When the same waitress walked up to take her order, Lana figured she had nothing to lose. Lana looked up at the woman and saw the name on her badge read Mable. "Mable, what is your special for the day? You do have one don't you?"

"Yeah, the special today is roast beef with carrots and potatoes; it comes with green beans and a salad."

"Okay, that sounds really good; I'll have that and just water to drink."

"Tea comes with the meal."

"Oh, really, well, I guess go ahead and bring me that too." Lana watched as the gum chewing waitress walked over to the counter and handed in her request. Now all she had to do was get the waitress talking and try to find out what she could about Luther's ex-wife.

When the waitress brought her a glass of iced tea, Lana put on her best smile, "By the way, you wouldn't happen to know a Luther Johnson would you?"

The waitress looked at her pityingly. "You shouldn't mention Luther around this café. If you are his latest I feel sorry for you."

"You know him?"

"I know of him, makes a difference. My friend Sophie is his ex-wife. He left her high and dry with two kids to raise. The boy is going to be like his father—no good, but we all have hopes for the little girl. Your order won't be much longer."

"All right, thanks." Lana sat very still for a moment; finally a lead, a genuine lead to the man. Now all she had to do was get the waitress to talk some more. Maybe she knew more than she was telling. She could find out when this Sophie came to work, and maybe she could talk to her. Surely she would have some idea where he could be found. He might even be at her house. That would be the very best news of all. If he could sweet talk her once, he could probably sweet talk her again.

Mable put the plate with her meal on the table in front of her, and started to move away. "Oh, this looks really good. Do you have a minute; I would like to ask you some more questions about your friend Sophie."

"Sorry, I have to keep moving, the boss don't like us chatting up the customers."

"But surely it would be all right for just a question or two."

Mable looked around and shrugged. "What do you want to know?"

"When does Sophia come to work, or is she here now?"

"She works the night shift. Comes to work about five or so, but if I were you I wouldn't be asking her about Luther. She gets might testy when his name is mentioned."

A man on one of the other tables banged his glass on his table. "See, can't chat; enjoy your meal." Mable turned away from Lana's table and began harassing the customer. They seemed to know each other and he was giving her a hard time about staying too long at every table but his. She gave as good as she got, and Lana wondered how the waitress could put up with people talking to her like the man did. That was one thing she hated about men; they all thought they hung the moon and women should kneel at their feet. Well, this was one old gal that would never ever kneel at any man's feet. She would make her own way in this world. She would never depend solely on the male of the species like her mother.

Lana looked after the waitress, and couldn't think of any other way to get the woman to stay and tell her any more she figured she might as well eat her meal and head home. She chewed thoughtfully on the roast beef, maybe she had enough. Maybe she should come back tonight and chat up the ex-wife. She smiled briefly, she'd find the elusive Luther Johnson or her name wasn't Lana Jacob.

Henry pulled into a parking place in front of the building that housed Hamilton Investigation. He got out of his automobile and strolled up to the building and climbed the stairs. He opened the door into the office and smiled at Roberta busily typing a letter.

"Hey," Henry said quietly.

Roberta looked up from her typing and smiled at him. "Hey, yourself, what are you doing back so soon?"

"You want me to turn around and wait a while?"

"No, silly, I just wasn't expecting you to get any information worth sharing so quickly. Did you find out anything?"

"Yeah, I did, I thought I would run it by you and Kathleen before I went to Sheriff Young about what I found out. I think I want you to tell me I'm crazy."

"Let me get Kathleen." Roberta picked up the receiver and dialed a couple of numbers. "Hey, Henry's back and he wants to tell us something. Okay."

Henry could hear a door open and footsteps tapping down the hallway. Kathleen came in and smiled at Henry and shook his hand.

"Roberta said you have some information?"

"Maybe, I talked with one of my fishing buddies, and he gave me some information about the victim and about Luther Johnson."

"We probably should go to my office to hear this, follow me."

"Wait I want to hear it too," Roberta said.

"Okay, but let's sit down. What do you have for us?"

Henry filled the two women in on what Matt told him and his take on the information.

"What do you think?" Henry asked.

Kathleen leaned back in her chair and put her finger tips together. "That does put a new light on everything doesn't it?"

"Yeah, I didn't think anything about seeing Phillip on the road, and really with everything else that has happened I had completely forgotten all about it, but with the new information about his dad; it does make you wonder."

"I would hate to accuse someone of murder without more to go on than you have. It could really be just a case of being in the wrong place at the wrong time," Kathleen said.

"I wouldn't have thought Phillip would have been involved in something like murder," Roberta said.

"You know Phillip?" Henry asked. Was that a jealous bone raising its head, he wondered.

"Just from school, he got into a bad group, it was all over school. Henry, you probably know more about it than I do," Roberta pulled a strand of hair forward and started curling it around her finger. "One of my friends was kind of sweet on him that is until he got in trouble, and then she turned to someone else to be loony over."

"I think the police have looked at him for petty theft, he's never done any time as far as I am aware. This would have been a major step up for him if he committed murder."

"I wonder if he would kill someone for his dad. According to the programs on TV, people kill for a lot of reasons," Roberta mused.

"Wait right there. I think we're jumping to conclusions. Just because Phillip was walking away from where the body was found doesn't mean he knew anything about it. He may have a perfectly good explanation. He may have been to see his dad," Kathleen argued. "Didn't you say that your source thought he might be in an abandoned house not for from the creek?"

"That's what he said. He knows the area better than I do. He's lived in and around here all of his life."

"But what if Phillip's dad was the one who murdered that Whitney guy?" Roberta asked.

"There is that." Kathleen said. "Henry, I think you should go over to the sheriff's office, and if Sheriff Young is there, you can give him your information and he can decide how to use it. I think this is bigger than anything Roberta or I can do. Oh, by the way, tell Sheriff Young that the pastor is sending Linda's picture over night to him, and she is definitely not home yet. He called and when she didn't answer, he sent someone over to check on the house. No one was there and from what he was able to get from the neighbors; no one had been home for at least three or four weeks."

"I'll be sure and tell him, you know I started to go there first, but I decided to come here. I sure don't want to get anyone in trouble."

"I think you should talk with Phillip first," Roberta said.

"Why," Kathleen asked.

"You said it; he may have a perfectly good explanation of why he was where Henry saw him."

Henry looked at Roberta and smiled. "And if he killed Whitney, do you think he'll tell me?"

"No, of course he won't. I just think…I don't know, he's a Kangaroo, we shouldn't throw him under the bus without an explanation."

"So now I'm to feel sorry for him because he graduated from Weatherford High School?" Henry smiled at Robert and saw her pleading eyes. He threw up his hands. "I'll think about it," Henry said as he got up and headed out the door.

Chapter 9

After Henry had visited with the sheriff, he headed out to A & W Root Beer drive-in. He slowed down but didn't see Matt's old pickup in the lot; so he kept driving. When he got back to the marina, he spotted Matt's pickup. He sat for a moment before he got out trying to decide what he wanted to ask Matt. If he pushed too hard, Matt might stop talking about Luther Johnson, and he wouldn't get any more information, but something told him that Matt knew more than he had told him.

Henry got out of his vehicle and started toward the marina. He looked around inside the marina and didn't see Matt anywhere. "Hey, you know where Matt is?" Henry asked Mr. Houston.

"He bought some bait and said he was going to fish in the fishing shed," Mr. Houston said. "What you want him for?"

"Nothing much; I understand you had an interesting visitor this morning."

"Are you talking about that lady that came here asking her questions?"

"Yeah, Matt didn't think much of her."

"Well, I can't say as I did either. Ole Blevins tried to sweet talk her into giving him the fifty bucks she offered, but she was too smart to fall for his line. I told him, if he wanted to earn some money, I could put him to work." Mr. Houston broke out in a laugh. "Didn't take him long to skedaddle. I ain't seen him move that fast since he started coming around here."

Henry joined in the laughter. "Are you telling me he wasn't interested in a job?"

"I hope you meant that sarcastically, he doesn't have any job at all as far as I know. I haven't figured out how he has any money. You know what's weird? When he started coming around here, oh I don't know, maybe six months or so ago, he asked about Luther Johnson also."

"Really, that seems strange."

"Struck me as strange at the time, Blevins hasn't lived here in a number of years."

"Matt said in at least a month of Sundays, I wonder why Blevins wanted to know about Luther."

"Your guess is as good as mine."

"You know I might as well ask you while I'm here," Henry pulled out Whitney's picture, "have you seen this man around here?"

Mr. Houston took the picture and stared at it. "This looks like a mug shot."

"I think it is."

"Yeah I've seen him. Not like yesterday, but about a couple of weeks ago, I think. Is it important?"

"I'm not sure. He turned up dead yesterday out by that creek on the east side of the lake."

"Is that what your brother called the sheriff about yesterday?"

"Yep, did he ask about Luther too?"

"Yeah, he did as a matter of fact. For a man who never made much of his life and that no one has seen since forever, Luther sure is popular."

"It would seem so, thanks for the information. I'm going to find Matt, see you around."

"You take it easy, you hear?"

Henry waved his hand as he headed out of the marina and started toward the shed that was built out into the water for the fishermen. He wondered why Blevins had been asking about Luther Johnson, for that matter why had Whitney asked about him. Now there was a woman asking about Luther. Were the two connected? It seemed strange that after ten or so years there are suddenly three people very interested in one man, and Whitney who had known Luther was found murdered. The time line didn't pan out. It didn't make any sense, shaking his head, he continued on his way. He opened the door and saw Matt and a couple of other men fishing at the end of the shed. Henry walked quietly up to him and touched his shoulder. Matt gave a start and started to snarl at Henry until he saw who it was.

"You sure gave me a start. What you up to? I didn't figure I'd see you again today."

"I wanted to talk to you some more about Luther Johnson."

"Huh, I think I told you everything I know about him."

"I just had a talk with Mr. Houston and he told me that Mr. Blevins was asking about him some time ago and Whitney, the murdered man, was asking about Luther Johnson also."

"Why the hell would Blevins be asking about Luther? I wouldn't think he even knew Luther. Unless…" Matt stared down at his fishing rod and muttered to himself. "You know that picture you showed me, well I think that dude was the con-man that Luther hung around with just before Luther left town. Luther never was real bright, but I thought he was smarter than to get caught up in a scam like that dude was running. It could have something to do with that, I guess. Maybe that Whitney was looking for Luther to help him start up the scam again."

"You think it's possible that some of the people who got scammed are after Luther? How much did you know about the scam?"

"Not a lot, Luther asked me to invest in it, but I don't have that kind of money. Never did. I told him to go climb a tall tree and not come down. He just laughed and said I'd be sorry I didn't invest in whatever he was selling. Never did figure it out completely."

"Was it a pyramid scheme?"

"Yeah, that's the word, pyramid. I told him only the guys at the top make any money and the peons on the bottom wouldn't make a dime. He got really mad at me and I never saw him again."

"Did you know that Whitney killed someone?"

"Yeah, I heard tell he did, but not Luther; he wouldn't kill anyone, or at least I don't think he would." Matt frowned in thought. "I guess anyone would kill if pushed far enough."

"You really think Luther could be hiding out here?"

"Anything's possible; could be why so many people are asking about him. I told you Luther isn't real bright. He's like a homing pigeon, always coming home to roost. "

"Okay, I thought maybe you had seen him around and hadn't wanted to say anything about it."

"Nah, he's not been around me; one thing is for sure he wouldn't come by my house or nothing."

"I'm curious, why wouldn't he?"

"I might have been his friend once, but since we had our row, not so much. You might check with his ex, I think she works the night shift at Jack's Café."

"I just might do that. I'm concerned about Luther, mainly because Whitney was found dead on Labor Day and if Luther was involved with him; he may be next on the list."

"Whitney's dead? Wow, I didn't realize that, you didn't say anything about it when you showed me his picture. Was he found here at the lake?"

"Yes, my baby brother found the body."

"I tell you what, if I hear anything or Luther contacts me, I'll let you know."

"Thanks, I appreciate that."

The men shook hands and Henry turned and hurried out of the shed. He settled in his car and went over everything he had learned from Matt. It wasn't much, but he decided that he would stop in at Jack's tonight and see what Luther's ex had to tell him. He smiled slowly, and he wondered if he could talk Roberta into coming with him. He started up the car, pulled out of the lot and headed back into town.

Roberta had been excited when Henry had asked her to go to dinner with him. She even wore a dress. The round neck, capped sleeve dress looked good on her, if she did say so herself, and the light blue color of the dress complimented her eyes. Henry hadn't said much since he had picked her up and she began to wonder if he regretted asking her out; after all he had just graduated from college not high school like she had.

Roberta cleared her throat. "Where are we going to eat?"

Henry glanced over at her and smiled. That smile made her heart do flips. "I thought we would go to Jack's. I hope that's okay."

"I guess, I don't think I have ever been there. Isn't it a truck stop or something?"

"Or something; I have an ulterior motive. You see after I left Sheriff Young today I went back to the lake. I talked with Matt again and he mentioned that

Luther's ex works the evening shift at Jack's. I thought maybe we could talk with her."

"So…"

"I know, I know, but I thought I needed an excuse to call you. I know you had just broken up with Eddy and I didn't know if you were ready to move on. I thought that if you turned me down I could dangle the chance to talk with Luther's ex before your eyes."

Roberta laughed and raised her eyebrows. "You didn't need an excuse to ask me out."

Henry glanced at Roberta again. "No?"

"No, I was hoping that you might get around to asking me out sometime. I'm not very faithful am I?"

"What do you mean?"

"Eddy breaks up with me this morning and I'm out with you tonight."

"Works for me, I have wanted to ask you out for some time but Eddy was in the way and I didn't want him accusing me of stealing his girl from him."

"You didn't. I am ready to move on and you are who I am ready to move on with."

"That's good to know."

"Now, let's get back to why we're going to Jack's; do you really think she may be able to tell us anything?"

"I'm not sure; probably not. Matt said that Luther hasn't been around here in quite some time, so it's possible she hasn't seen or heard from him. The thing is it won't hurt to ask."

"Do you still think Luther may have killed that guy we found?"

"I'm not sure what to think. Matt said that he didn't think Luther would kill anyone. He claimed Luther might steal or run a scam on someone, but he didn't think he would commit murder."

"You never know, you hear people on TV claiming that the guy next door that was arrested for murder was such a nice guy. He was even kind to dogs and cats."

"Yeah, I know, but Matt did point out that everyone will kill if given the right motive."

"Whee, that gives me cold chills. What you're saying is that old man Hansen down the street could be a murderer."

"Since I don't know Mr. Hansen, I won't comment. But I think he's right, if pushed hard enough anyone might kill someone, but someone like you and I would probably not ever get over it. It's only the bad guys who continue to kill and have no regrets." Henry slowed down and turned into Jack's parking lot.

"It looks like a good crowd tonight," Roberta said as she stared at all the cars parked in the lot combined with a few semis.

"I hope we can get a table in Sophia's section," Henry said as he opened his door. He went around and opened Roberta's door and helped her out.

"Sophia, is that her name?"

"Yes, at least that is what Matt said it was." They walked slowly into the building and waited on someone to seat them.

A young girl in her twenties came up with some menus in her hands. "Just two?"

"Yes, and is it possible to be seated in Sophia Johnson's section?" Henry said.

"Hum, let me see." She looked at her book and then looked around at the tables. "If you don't mind a booth, I think I can seat you in her section."

"A booth is fine. Thank you," Henry looked at Roberta for conformation. Roberta nodded her head.

"Follow me."

Once they were seated, Henry looked around and wrinkled his nose. "Not a very classy place to bring a lady on a date."

"Hey, it's better than Dairy Queen. I've never actually been brought to a sit-down café with a date. It's usually Dairy Queen or A & W. I mean, neither of those places is bad, but it gets kinda old."

Henry smiled. "I think I can do better than that most of the time."

"Good evening, are you ready to order?" Sophia asked as she pushed her bleached blonde hair back behind her ear and gave a tired sigh.

"Oh, we're not quite ready, but you can bring us a drink. I'd like an iced tea. What about you, Roberta?"

"I'll have tea also." Roberta smiled a big smile.

"They'll be right out."

Roberta watched Sophia walk away. "She sure looks tired, but I would think working at a place like this and having to listen to complaints and bitching would make anyone tired."

"It's one of the few places that a woman can make enough to live on, especially if she has kids and no husband."

Roberta shook her head. "I certainly plan to go to college and if nothing else get a degree so I can teach."

Sophia came back with the drinks and sat them down. "Are you ready to order?"

"Oh, yes," Henry said in confusion. He had been concentrating on Roberta so much that he hadn't even looked at the menu.

They gave their orders and before Sophia could turn away, Henry jumped in with a question.

"Miss Johnson, I was wondering if you had heard from your ex-husband lately."

The frozen stare he got should have put ice in his veins. Henry swallowed hard and waited.

"Luther, I haven't heard from him in at least ten years. A good thing too, if it's another ten years, I'll be happy. Now I have to turn your order in." Sophia turned and headed away from their table as fast as she could walk.

"Boy, you made an impression," Roberta said with a laugh.

"I sure hit a nerve didn't I. She knew exactly how long Luther has been gone and did you notice she didn't say he wasn't here; only that she hadn't heard from him. Maybe I should try to talk with Phillip."

"Do you think Phillip may have heard from him and she is trying to protect him?"

"It's possible, I won't know until I speak with him. I'll try to track him down tomorrow. In the mean time let's talk about you."

"Silly, I'm not interesting."

"You might be surprised just how interesting you are."

Chapter 10

Linda paced the small room restlessly, turning when she reached a wall, and then turning sharply to head back toward another wall. She couldn't recall how long she had been locked in this room. It was small, only big enough for a bed and dresser if there had been a dresser. The days and nights were all running together. A man with a gun came in three times a day and brought her food and took her to the bathroom. That timed her day, the nights were endless because she would sleep and wake up and do the routine all over again. In the beginning Walter had been with her, encouraging her to think positive and not be frightened. He swore they would be able to get away; he had assured her that he would be able to talk the men into letting them go, but a day or two ago the man with a gun came and took Walter away. Before he left he had held her in his arms, promised he wouldn't be gone long and they would leave then. She hadn't seen him since. When she asked about him, the man just shrugged.

She kept telling herself that everything would be all right; that Walter would return any minute, but a couple of nights ago, she had felt something, she wasn't sure what it was, but an emptiness, a bad emptiness. At that moment she knew that Walter was dead, whether he had been killed she didn't know, but she knew he was dead. She had worked up her courage and asked about him when one of the men had taken her to the bathroom, but he had ignored her. She hadn't bothered asking again; because she knew in her bones Walter was dead. If she dwelt on the knowledge, she would start to cry, so she waited with patience for them to kill her also.

Linda sat down on the double bed which was the only furniture in the room. There wasn't even a chair or a table. The one small window was nailed shut and the panes were too small for a person to get through. Walter had checked all of that out when they had first been brought here. She told him when they first left Huntsville that going to Dallas was a mistake. She told him she had a bad feeling about the trip, but he had been adamant about going. She still didn't understand why.

Everything was great when they first got there. They drove around and saw the sights, they moved on to Fort Worth to take in the zoo and the museums. Then one night a little weasel of a man showed up at their hotel room. She remembered having seen him one time at the prison. She knew he and Walter had been cell mates and had been one of the men that Walter had her check where he had gone. She didn't like him on sight and hoped he wouldn't stay long. His dirty brown hair had been pulled back in a pony tail and his eyes never stopped moving. Later Walter told her he had been high on heroin. The two men went down to the lobby leaving her alone in the room, and when Walter came back up, he was really excited. He wouldn't tell her what they had discussed, and even got angry at her when she continued to ask about it. Walter told her that he was going to leave her here at the hotel and make a side trip to a small town called Weatherford. He assured her he wouldn't be gone long and when he got back they would head back to Huntsville. He didn't stay gone long, not even a whole day, and when he mentioned going back, they began to argue again, she hadn't wanted him to leave her in Fort

Worth. It was just too big and scary, nothing like home. In the middle of their argument someone knocked on the door. Walter opened it to find three men with guns standing in the doorway. They had pushed their way into the room and seemed surprised to see that Walter wasn't alone. To give Walter credit he tried to talk them out of taking both of them, but it hadn't fazed them. Now she was locked in this little room, knowing in her heart Walter was dead and she would be next.

His words continued to run circles in her mind, *"Don't worry, honey, this has to do with some old business. I'll take care of it. It's nothing for you to worry about."* She fell back onto the bed, her hands over her face. She felt the tears trickle down the side of her face, and soak into the bed covers. They were going to kill her, and she was scared, so very scared. She had tried praying, but the prayers never seemed to reach higher than the ceiling. *"God, were are you? Help me! Please help me!"*

Two men sat at a table; cards in their hands and money in front of them. Their suit coats and ties were draped on the back of their chairs, but they still wore their shoulder holsters. One of the men threw his cards on the table in disgust.

"You win again, this just isn't my night," the heavy-built man named John said. His dark brown hair stood up in a flat top and it glistened from the wax that he wore on it.

Teddy took the cigar out of his mouth and grinned. "I told you I was on a roll today. Don't worry you'll win it back tomorrow." Teddy pushed his bulk out of his chair and headed to the make-shift kitchen in the corner of the room. His footsteps thudded loudly on the wooden floors as he walked to the refrigerator that sat in the corner humming quietly.

Teddy opened the refrigerator and looked over his shoulder. "You want a beer?"

John stood up and stretched. "Sure, why not, nothing else to do in this godforsaken place; I wonder when Frank and Jimmy will be back."

"Your guess is as good as mine. I hope it's soon, I'm getting hungry."

"Me too, I hope the boss ends this soon," John said as he went to a window and stared out at the weed infested yard. "I don't see any use hanging out here with nothing to do. I can't see that the broad is of any use, and obviously she doesn't know anything."

"The money's good, but you're right it is boring. I'm ready to move on to something a little more exciting." Teddy put the beer bottles under the opener attached to the wall and opened each one. He strolled over to his friend and handed him one of the beers.

John put his finger against his lips as he flattened his body against the wall next to the window. Teddy did the same on the other side of the window. They both listened to the car wheels coming down the lane to the house. "Jimmy and Frank do you think?" Teddy asked almost in a whisper.

John glanced quickly out the window and shook his head. "It's an old pickup truck, the boss maybe?"

The two men relaxed and waited as they each took a swig of their beer. A loud bang of an automobile door closing broke the silence, and then heavy footsteps came thudding up the broken down porch steps. "Open up," a gruff voice said.

John went over and unlocked the brand new lock that had been put on the old door. He pulled the door open and ushered the man in who was waiting on the other side.

A heavy-set man of about forty sauntered into the room. He was dressed in overalls and brogans. His plaid shirt was rolled up on his beefy arms. Taking his sunglasses off, he looked over at each of the men and shook his head. "That had better be the first beer of the day. I'm not paying you to drink on the job. By the way, how is our guest?"

"She's fine," John answered as he closed and relocked the door. "We're waiting on Jimmy and Frank to show up with dinner so we can feed her. She ain't any problem; just sat there on the bed and stays completely away from us when we bring her food to her. If she hadn't seen us we could probably let her go. I'm not big on whacking women."

"No one asked you to, the thing is if you hadn't brought her along you wouldn't have to worry about whacking her."

"Hey, not our fault," John said.

"Never mind that now, we got a problem," the boss said.

"What kind of problem," Teddy asked as he sat down.

"They've already found the body. I thought I told you guys to carry it into Tarrant County."

"We took it as far from here as we could without going into Tarrant County. Nobody ever goes anywhere near that creek," John said.

"Well, they did on Labor Day."

"What do you mean? We didn't dump him right on the road, we took him quite a ways off the road and dumped him in some tall weeds next to that creek." John sat down and took a swallow of beer. "That dude should have been good until the crows or wild animals found him."

"A bunch of kids found him. Don't ask me how and now there are people asking about him and his lady.

We'll have to get rid of her and make sure she's not ever found. And to put the frosting on the cake, so to speak, there's people asking about Luther Johnson. Of course, if we can't find him, I don't much worry about anyone else finding him before I can get my hands on him."

"Don't worry boss, no one can connect the dead body to us," Teddy said. "We made sure to strip him of his ID. It'll be weeks before they figure out who he is."

The boss turned and stared at Teddy. "You really think so? You stupid ass, Sheriff Young may be the sheriff of a hick town, but he has more'n two brain cells in his head. According to what I heard, they already know who he is, and now they are looking for the wife. I was told you four were the best," the boss said as he stopped his pacing and stared at the two men sitting at ease at the poker table.

"We are the best," John said as he sat up straight and glared at the man who was staring at him accusingly. "If anyone says different, they're lying."

"You've bungled this from the start. You were supposed to bring me Walter Whitney, not he and his wife, and now you can't even find Luther Johnson."

Teddy looked over at his friend and cleared his throat. "We couldn't get one without the other. She never left him alone. We waited and waited; finally we decided that we'd just grab them both. You know, after she had seen us we had to bring her along."

"I told you to wait. Sooner or later he would have gone out without her. Now you're going to have to kill her and that wasn't part of my plan."

"You know I told you I don't like killing women, but I can do it. Maybe I'll get Jimmy to do it. Since his old lady stiffed him, he's been down on women. It's almost like he hates them; all of them. So we'll take care of it for you," John said as he sat his empty beer bottle down hard.

"Like you took care of disposing of Whitney's body, I don't think so. I don't need to clean up anymore of your messes. Maybe I should just do my own dirty work and not pay you two anymore." The boss had paced down to the far wall of the little house and as he turned around he held a 22 revolver in his hand.

Teddy gave a snort. "What you going to do with that little pea-shooter? You think me and John, here, is afraid of your little gun?" Teddy pulled out his 38 and pointed it at his boss. "Mine makes a bigger hole than yours does and I don't miss."

A loud shot rang out and Teddy slumped over in his chair and fell to the floor. The boss swung toward John who had started pulling out his own gun. "Don't even go there," the boss snarled, "or you'll be next."

"Hell, you killed him. Why did you go and do that? We were just following your orders; there was no call to shoot him."

"You think not? I wouldn't be too sure of that if I were you. You may be next. Now get him out of here."

John stared up at the man that he and his friends had laughed at and called a pantywaist. He had just shot his friend without blinking an eye. It didn't seem to even affect him; now he stood holding his gun loosely and seemed to be waiting for him to make a move. Then John heard another car coming up the lane toward the house. Hopefully this would be Jimmy and Frank, and it would be three against this maniac.

Chapter 11

Roberta smiled a big smile as she prepared for bed. The dinner date with Henry was so much fun, and she didn't even have to fight him off. When he took her home, he did kiss her; and what a kiss. Her smile got even bigger. "Hum," she thought, she could handle more of that kind of kissing. She slipped into her baby-doll pajamas and snuggled under her covers. He had asked for a date for Saturday night and she could hardly wait.

Her smile dimmed as she thought about their conversation with Mrs. Johnson. She had certainly not been forth-coming. She hoped Henry would take her with him when he went to speak with Phillip, but of course if it was during the day she wouldn't be able to go. Her dad wanted her to get all of her typing and filing done before next week. She knew that there was more work now that Kathleen was doing investigations too, but even with that she didn't know how Kathleen had kept up.

She fell asleep almost immediately, dreaming of weddings in June, but then her dreams turned to nightmares, dead men with ants covering them holding out their arms to her, and she had to brush them off, but she couldn't reach them. She sat straight up in bed breathing hard with tears running down her face; she still couldn't move her legs; she fought for a minute still trapped in the nightmare. She looked down and saw her legs tangled in the sheet, and realized her body was wet from perspiration. She got up quietly not wanting to wake Darlene, and headed to the kitchen. She had to get a drink of water; she had to walk off this nightmare. She stood at the sink sipping the water, trying to get her breathing under control.

"Roberta, are you all right?" Sarah asked.

"I'm fine, Mom. I needed a drink of water," Roberta whispered as she turned toward her mom.

"This isn't like you, so I know something is wrong. You might as well tell me."

Roberta looked down at her hand holding the glass of water. Her body quivered, she took a deep breath, and tried to push away the dreams. "I kept dreaming about that dead man we found except it wasn't him in my dream."

"Who was it?

"I don't want to talk about it." Roberta turned away from her mom and put the glass into the sink.

Sarah came over and put her arms around Roberta. "Dear, sometimes it helps if you talk about it."

Roberta shook her head. "I don't think so. It really freaked me out. It wasn't just one man it was several different people. I kept trying to wake them up and get the ants off of them, but I couldn't." She gave a soft sob. "Don't you understand I couldn't get the ants off?"

"Oh, dearest, it's all right. You're right; don't think about it anymore."

"But what if it's a premonition or something, what if what I dreamed comes true?"

"Who did you keep seeing?"

"Henry, Carl, Eddy and lastly Janice, all of them, oh Mom it was awful; I was afraid to wipe the ants off the last body I saw, I was afraid it would be me."

Roberta buried her head in her mother's shoulder and sobbed.

Sarah stood holding her baby girl and wished she could make everything better like she had when Roberta was young. She was grown now and her mom could no longer make the bad things that happened in life go away. It was a shame that the four teenagers had found that dead body. She shook her head in disbelief at all that had happened to her girls this summer. First Darlene had been involved in a murder, then Patricia Ann. Since Kathleen had decided she wanted to be a private investigator, it would be only natural she might run into a dead body, which she did. Sarah didn't like it, but Kathleen was too old for her mom to tell her what to do. Roberta was different; she was only eighteen, just starting her life. Why did it have to happen to her baby girl?

"It's all right, honey, it will be all right." She knew the platitudes were meaningless, but that was all she could think to say.

Roberta pulled away from her mom and used the skirt of her baby-dolls to wipe her eyes. "I'm okay, really, I am. I guess if it hadn't been people I knew it wouldn't have affected me this way."

"Maybe you should go talk with Brother Bob."

Roberta shook her head. "Oh no, I'll be all right. It's weird I never dreamed about that body that we found in the old Vaughn house; so why now? It doesn't make sense."

"Who knows why you dreamed now and not then."

"I think it was the ants. That really bothered me for some reason. I think I could have handled it better if I had seen where birds or wild animals had gotten to him."

"Do you really? I think that would bother me more."

"Silly isn't it." Roberta took another deep breath. "Oh well, I should try to go back to sleep, I have a full day tomorrow, and guess what?"

Sarah smiled, "What?"

"Henry asked me out for Saturday night. I can hardly wait."

"You seem to enjoy going out with Henry more than his brother."

Roberta grinned and dipped her head. "Yeah, I really like him."

"Don't get in any hurry, you have college to get through, and you may meet a lot of men that you *really* like before you graduate."

"Maybe," Roberta said as her grin got bigger. "We'll see."

Shaking her head, Sarah followed Roberta as they went back to their bedrooms. Roberta stopped and hugged her mom. "Thanks for being there for me, just now. It made me feel so much better although I may not be able to go back to sleep." She went back to bed hoping the nightmare would not come back, and she fell into a dreamless sleep.

The next morning as she was eating breakfast, the telephone rang. Her mom answered it and handed the receiver to Roberta.

"It's for you, Henry I think," Sarah smiled at her baby girl and winked.

Roberta felt her face heat up with embarrassment as she took the receiver. "Hi, what's up?"

"Just thought I would call and see what your schedule is for today."

"I have tons of work to get through, why?"

"I am going to track down Phillip; if he's working I'll wait until after five to talk with him. I thought you might want to come along."

"Oh, yes, I definitely do, so make it after five."

"Why don't I pick you up at the office?"

"Sure, I can ride in with Kathleen or Dad."

"I'll see you then."

With a big smile, Roberta stood up and replaced the receiver on the base of the wall phone. She picked up her plate and put it in the sink. Turning to Kathleen who was still eating, she asked, "Can I ride to the office with you today?"

"Sure," Kathleen said with a smile. "Have you got a hot date for supper?"

"You might say that, Henry is picking me up."

"Don't be out late," Robert said as he picked up his jacket and headed out.

"I won't, I promise," Roberta said as she watched her dad leave by the door leading into the garage.

"If you want to wear something more casual on your date, grab you some clothes while I go brush my teeth. I won't be but a minute."

"Thanks, I think I will." Roberta hurried to her room and grabbed a set of cloths at random including a pair of tennis shoes.

Going into the office Kathleen glanced over at Roberta. "You seem to be getting serious about Henry kind of fast. I mean, Eddy has just dumped you, are you sure this isn't rebound?"

"I don't think so, I've been thinking about asking Eddy to cool it and agree that we date other people. The thing was I never could get nerve enough to actually have 'the talk,'" she raised her hands and did quotes, "with Eddy. Just a coward I guess. It shook me up when he broke it off, I think mainly because I had been such a coward that I couldn't do it. I was afraid of hurting his feelings, I guess. Now I feel free to go out with whomever I want, and I want to date Henry." Roberta looked down at her clenched fists and then back up at her sister. "Do you think Eddy will freak when he finds out we are dating?"

"Hum, good question, I would suppose you will have to wait and find out won't you?"

"I was afraid you were going to say that. It should have been me that broke it off, don't you think?"

"I have a feeling if you had broken it off; it would have been worse. No one, especially a little brother or sister likes to think they have been replaced by an older sibling. Since Eddy broke it off; he can't accuse you of having done it so you could go with his older brother."

"Changing the subject, Henry is going to try to find Phillip Johnson today and if he does we're going to talk with him about his dad."

"Why do you want to talk with Phillip Johnson?"

"His dad's name keeps coming up in this. His dad was involved with the dead guy in a con they ran, and now all of a sudden several people are asking about him."

"Have you talked with the sheriff about this?"

"Only what Henry found out yesterday morning. He talked with Sheriff Young then. We went to Jacks last night for supper and spoke with Phillip's mom and she claimed she hadn't seen her ex."

"You need to be careful, you hear?"

"I will, I don't want to end up like you with some crazy pointing a gun at me. That would be beyond scary."

"It's not pleasant, I can tell you."

Roberta had been waiting all day for five o'clock and it finally came. Her dad had left the office a few minutes ago and now Kathleen was waiting with her for Henry to come pick her up. "You can go on home," Roberta said as she put the cover on her typewriter and started straightening her desk for the night.

"I'll leave as soon as Henry gets here. If I get home and I tell Mom and Dad that I left you here, I would have to come back. You know how they are."

"He'll be here soon. He called about four and said he might be a little late. He had to run an errand for his dad."

"Still, this office can be really spooky when there is no one here but you. I have heard footsteps, voices; all kinds of noises. Trust me you don't want to be here alone, especially after dark."

"Is this place haunted? That is so cool."

"Silly, there is no such thing as ghosts, haven't you figured that out yet? I think it is just your imagination gets the better of you when you're alone."

"Okay, I appreciate you staying. I'm sure he'll be here soon."

The phone rang breaking the silence that had fallen on the sisters. Roberta picked up the receiver. "Good afternoon, Hamilton Investigations, this is Roberta speaking, how may I help you?"

"Oh, oh okay. Yes, I understand, I'll go on home with Kathleen. Yes, we can make it another day."

She hung up the phone and looked at her sister with tears in her eyes. "That was someone calling for Henry, and breaking our date. I don't understand. At four, we were still on."

"It wasn't Henry that called?"

Roberta shook her head as she wiped the tears from her eyes. "It was some friend of his, I didn't catch the name. I-I guess we can leave now." Roberta got up and pulled her purse out of the lower desk drawer.

"Something came up I'm sure. He'll call tonight."

"You know, I don't even care," Roberta said through her tears, with her head held high. "I hope he never calls again. I don't like a man who breaks dates at the last minute. Eddy may not have been exciting, but at least he never broke a date."

"You go, little sister," Kathleen said as she gave Roberta a quick hug. "I forgot something I need in my office. I won't be but a minute."

"Okay, I'll go to the bathroom while you are doing that."

When Kathleen got to her office, she did a quick search in the phone book and dialed a number. "Hello, is Henry there?"

"No, he left about five minutes ago. He has a date. Who may I tell him has called?"

"Is this his mother?"

"Yes, who is this?"

"This is Kathleen Hamilton, he had a date with my younger sister and she just got a call breaking that date. I was just curious."

"Oh, Kathleen, he was headed to your office. I understand Roberta is working there for your dad."

"You say he left about five minutes ago?"

"Yes, he should be there soon, that is unless the train stops him."

"Thanks. I won't keep you."

"Give my regards to your parents."

"Will do."

Kathleen hung up the receiver and stood staring into space. The door opened behind her, startling her.

"Are you ready?" Roberta asked.

"What, oh, sure, I'll just use the bathroom before we leave. Why don't you make sure everything is closed down; you know coffee pot, etc.?"

"Okay."

After Kathleen had killed as much time as she could, she headed to the reception area. "I guess we can leave now."

"I'm ready," Roberta said quietly.

They locked up and headed down the stairs to the sidewalk. Roberta came to an abrupt halt when they reached the sidewalk.

"Look there's Henry's car," she said pointing her finger.

"Well, what do you know; he didn't break your date after all."

"But where is he? It doesn't look like anyone is in the car." Roberta turned toward Kathleen with a worried frown on her face.

The two girls walked quickly toward Henry's car and Roberta peered inside and gave a short scream. "Oh, no, oh no," she repeated over and over again as she backed up.

"What is it?" Kathleen asked as she looked in the car. "Oh my goodness, wait here I'll go call an ambulance."

"It's just like the dead man, hurry, please hurry."

"Don't touch anything," Kathleen called as she ran back to the office.

Roberta heard the sirens before Kathleen got back. She was afraid to open the door, afraid to touch

Henry, afraid he was dead. Tears streamed down her face and she jumped when Kathleen put her arm around her.

"They are on the way. Here's Sheriff Young now."

"What's going on?" Sheriff Young asked in a gruff voice moving swiftly toward the two girls.

Roberta didn't say anything, she just pointed to the car where Henry lay in the front seat.

Sheriff Young opened the door and felt for a pulse. "He's still alive, but the pulse is weak. We definitely need to get him to the hospital." He turned to Roberta. "What have you two been up to?"

"Nothing, I promise, nothing. He and I had a date tonight and when he didn't show up I decided to go home with Kathleen. We saw-we saw his car and came to see what was going on and then we found him like that. I was afraid to touch anything."

"Now don't you worry here comes the ambulance, we'll get him to the hospital as soon as we can. Kathleen, why don't you take your sister on home, I'll let you know how he is."

"I think that is a good idea. Come on Roberta let's go home."

Roberta started shaking her head. "No, oh no, I want to go to the hospital with him. Please Kathleen; please take me to the hospital. I can't stand not know how he is, and—I don't know, I just want to be there."

"It won't hurt anything," Sheriff Young said motioning toward the ambulance driver. "Hey over here guys, he's in the front seat. He's still alive so take him straight to Campbell; I'll be right behind you."

Chapter 12

The shot vibrated through the small house. Linda jumped up from the bed and her eyes darted from side to side, looking for a place to hide. Where had the shot come from, she wondered franticly? She knew she wasn't hurt so no one had shot at her. Her eyes continued to roam over the room searching and not finding a hiding place. The only place was under the bed, and it would be the first place they would look. Her body trembled and sobs were coming fast and furious. She had to hide; she had to find some place safe, but there didn't seem to be any safe place. Fear had taken over and made her thoughts jumbled.

Her eyes fell on the old iron bedstead. It was against the wall pushed into a corner; if she could pull it out enough to get behind it, and into the far corner maybe she wouldn't be noticed. She struggled with the old bed, the adrenalin giving her the strength to move it away from the wall. A loud squeaking caused her to pause, but not for long. Flattening her body against the wall she managed to ease her way down the wall until she was in the corner of the room. She knelt down and lay on her side under the bed, and with both hands, she shoved the bed back into place. Linda then scooted into the corner by wrapping her arms around the leg of the bed, and curling into a ball. Trying to calm her sobs, she began to pray in earnest; begging the Lord to keep her hidden from her captures.

Silence reigned in the front room of the little house and the four men faced each other. Jimmy and Frank had entered the room and stopped as they took in the scene of their dead comrade, John and their boss.

"What in the world happened here?" Jimmy asked as he set down the sack of sandwiches he had in his hand.

"Your friend got too big for his britches. I had to take him down a notch or two," the boss said as he walked over and nudged the dead body with the toe of his shoe.

Frank walked over and set the drinks down on the table. "I'd appreciate it if you would let the rest of us know if we are as you say 'getting too big for our britches.' I don't wish to end up like Teddy there."

"Get rid of the body, but not where someone will find it the next day. I'm heading back to the marina to see what news I can pick up there."

"You want me to get rid of the broad?" John asked.

"Later, we might be able to use her at some point." The boss strolled uncaring out of the room, not even checking to see if one of the hired hoods would pull a gun on him.

Jimmy turned to John and scratched his head. "What in the world happened here? I realize the boss killed Teddy, but why?"

"The boss and Teddy had an argument and the boss won. The boss was pissed because Whitney's body was found the day after we dumped it. He claimed he wanted us to take it all the way to Tarrant County and of course we didn't."

"What difference did it make?" Frank asked. "We got rid of the body and no one will know who it is; nor will they connect it to us."

"I thought so too, but it seems the small town sheriff has more on the ball than we thought. The body has been identified. Also, someone is looking for Luther Johnson."

"Huh, well if the boss can shoot one of us; why doesn't he take care of his own dirty work?" Jimmy asked.

"He doesn't want to be arrested for the murder of anyone," Frank said.

"I think you hit the nail on the head. The boss wants to stay squeaky clean in all of this. If we're caught it will just be his word against ours," John said. He opened one of the sacks of food. "I'm hungry and since I can't do anything for Teddy I'm going to eat."

"Frank and I will take him outside. We can take care of him later," Jimmy said.

"Want me to take care of the little lady?" Frank asked.

"It'll wait until we get Teddy's body out of here," Jimmy said. "She ain't going anywhere."

"You know the boss may be on to something about other people looking for Luther Johnson. You remember yesterday when we were getting the food at Jacks; that lady came in asking about Luther," Frank said as he sat down.

"Who was it?" John asked.

"Not sure. She talked with the waitress and we couldn't hear what was being said. Then she ate her meal and left," Jimmy said. "I had forgotten about it until you mentioned it."

"Who knows who she was; she may have been an old girlfriend. She may have been the ex-wife," Frank said with a shrug.

"I know the waitress was put out that she had to talk about him," Jimmy said.

"Sounds like another dead end to me," John said.

"I'm going to take the gal her food and take her to the bathroom. I sure don't like letting her use that pail in there, when she does one of us has to empty it, and it smells something awful," Frank said. Frank rose from his chair and headed toward the locked door; the sandwich and drink in his hand. He unlocked it and walked in. Silence was deafening as he stood in the doorway looking around the room. He backed out and kicked the door shut.

Turning toward the other two men, Frank opened his mouth a couple of times before any words came out. "She-she ain't in there," Frank finally got out.

John got up and started toward the stunned man. "What you mean 'she ain't there'?"

"Just what I said; I opened the door and figured she would be on the bed, that's where she usually is and she's not on the bed; she's not anywhere. That room isn't big enough for her to hide. In fact there is no place to hide," Frank said as his eyes grew large. "You know what that idiot Whitney said."

"He was just saying stuff to get us all stirred up," John said.

"But she is gone. He said her God would take care of her. He spouted off something about Daniel in the lion's den and those three men in a fiery furnace. Maybe he knew what he was talking about," Frank said. His hands had begun to tremble and he quickly sat the food back on the table.

"And you believed him?" Jimmy asked.

"How do you explain her being gone? She ain't in there I tell you. She's gone."

"Now wait a minute," Jimmy said. "She has to be in there. Neither Teddy nor I took her out, and the only way she can get out is through that door. Just settle down and we'll figure this out," John said.

"We'll have a better look later," Frank said. "We should bury Teddy. I ain't throwing his body in some creek or roadside park. He was my friend and he deserves a burial."

"I agree with you. We can bury him in the back and the boss will never know the difference," Jimmy said.

"I'm with you guys. I think there is a shovel in that old shed in the back," John said.

The three men trooped out. Quiet settled on the little house and a very frightened woman, who lay huddled under the bed, slowly eased out of her hiding place. She stood up and tried to brush the dirt and dust bunnies off of her clothes. She tip-toed to the door and tried the door knob. She almost cried out when the knob turned in her hand. She eased the door open and peeked out. No one was in the room, at least no one alive. Linda moved as silently as she could across the room, turning her head so she wouldn't have to look at the dead man lying on the floor.

Tremors attacked her body, but she took a deep breath and continued on to the front door. If the men were out front, she would be doomed. She continued to pray and thank God that he had let her even get this far. If she could get away, she would have even more to thank Him for.

She glanced over at the table and saw the sack of food; she swerved to pick it up and continued toward the front door. It seemed like the door was a mile away, she didn't think she would ever get there. Finally, she had her hand of the door knob; turning it slowly and hoping it wouldn't make a noise. She had no idea where the men were. She just knew they weren't in the front room. They could be out on the porch smoking or something. She had heard them talking, but hadn't been able to tell what they had been saying. Easing the door open she didn't see anyone, but her eyes fastened on the unattended car. Would the keys be in it, she wondered? Would her luck still hold? She stopped momentarily as she closed the door. She ran down the porch steps, and glanced in the car as she went past it. Dangling from the ignition were the keys.

"Oh, thank you dear Lord," she whispered. She slowly and carefully opened the car door. She could hear the men in the back talking, she couldn't make out what they said, and it didn't matter; all that mattered was that she get the car started and get out of here before they realized she had escaped. Linda sat down in the seat and took a deep breath. So far, so good, she thought. Now would be the hard part. She pushed down the lock on her side and reached across the passenger seat and pushed down the lock there. She would just have to hope they wouldn't try the back doors.

With trembling hands, Linda turned the key and gave a sigh of relief when the car roared to life, and as she put it into gear, she kept praying, "Oh Lord, oh Lord, help me. Help me." Her hands were shaking so bad she could hardly turn the wheel to head the car down the dirt road. She heard shouts and running feet as she put the car in drive and floored the accelerator. She never looked back as she drove the big black car down the road; still praying and crying.

The three men came to a stop and looked at each other for a moment. "What the hell?" John said.

"We're in deep shit," Jimmy explained as he leaned forward to get his breath. "The boss will kill us all over this."

"You've got that right," Frank said.

"Didn't you lock the door after you checked it?" John asked.

"I thought I did. Where the hell was she hiding, I could have sworn there was no one in that room," Frank said.

"It won't matter what you thought, the boss is going to kill us all. If you hadn't noticed, he ain't too happy with us now," Jimmy said.

"I think once we get Teddy buried we need to high-tail it out of here," John said.

"That would be nice if we could, but if you haven't noticed we no longer have an automobile to high-tail it in," John said sarcastically.

"We'll find one, let's get Teddy buried and get our butts out of here before the boss comes back," Jimmy said.

"Just where do you think we'll find said car?" John asked and the men turned back to finish digging the hole behind the house.

"People leave their cars with the keys in them all the time or we'll hot wire it. We should get this done before dark; I don't relish being in these weeds and tall grass after dark," Jimmy said.

"You afraid of boogers?" Frank asked grinning.

"Not boogers, but I am afraid of rattlesnakes. I saw a big one back here the other day," Jimmy said.

"I'm with Jimmy; the boogieman I can handle but rattlesnakes are a different thing all together," John said as he picked up a rusty pick and started digging again.

Chapter 13

Henry lay with his eyes closed wondering why his head felt as if a Ball Peen hammer was battering his head. Why did it hurt so badly? Had he been on a seven day drunk? He tried to think but it hurt to think. He didn't think he had been on a drunk; it didn't feel like it. There was no foul taste in his mouth, and he didn't remember having anything to drink. What had he been doing? Suddenly, he realized his mind was blank. Wait a minute, he thought, I remember my name, right? It's Henry-Henry Miller, my parents are still alive and I have a younger brother, Eddy. A smile curved his lips, and I have started dating Roberta Hamilton.

So, he had the essentials, but why couldn't he remember where he was and why his head hurt so badly. He slowly lifted on eyelid and saw the snow white walls. He made the mistake of trying to turn his head, but stopped as a sharp pain stabbed through his head. Someone moaned, and he realized it was coming from him. A soft hand touched his.

"Henry, you're awake, thank goodness," Roberta said as she stroked his hand.

"Where-where am I?" Henry whispered. "My head—it hurts so badly."

"Your in Campbell Memorial," Roberta answered as she continued to stroke his hand.

"It hurts," he murmured.

"Your head, I'm sure it does. The doctor said you have a concussion, and that you are lucky."

"Don't feel lucky."

"I guess not, but the blow didn't crack the skull. Your dad said you have always had a very hard head."

"Are they here?"

"Your parents, not right now. Your dad took your mom to get something to eat."

"What-how long have I been out?"

"The ambulance brought you in last night about five-thirty. It's going on nine now."

"Nine in the morning?" Henry asked in surprise.

"Yes, nine in the morning; I'm going to ring for the nurse now, they wanted to know when you woke up."

"Wait, what happened?"

"Someone hit you really hard on the back of the head. I wanted to stay with you last night, but Dad pointed out that since your parents were here, my staying would be overkill. I came back about eight this morning and that's when your dad made your mom go with him to get something to eat."

"Why would someone hit me? Did they steal what little money I had on me?"

"No. You really don't remember anything do you?"

"Only my name, your name and my family, not why I'm here or why someone would try to kill me."

"Sheriff Young thinks it may have something to do with the questions you have been asking around the marina at Weatherford Lake."

"What kind of—Luther Johnson, I had been asking about Luther Johnson. Wait a minute, not just Luther Johnson, but I had questions about a Walter Whitney, too."

"See your memory is coming back. We were going to talk with Phillip, Luther Johnson's son last night."

Henry closed his eyes momentarily. Thoughts and images chased each other through his mind. He had found Phillip—where had he found Phillip? Why did he want to talk to him, why had he been asking questions about his dad? None of it made since. Walter Whitney—why did he need to ask questions about a man he didn't know? For that matter, why was he asking questions about Phillip and his dad?

"Henry, are you okay?" Roberta asked worriedly.

"Trying to think—hurts to think," Henry whispered. He felt as if he talked any louder it would cause his head to explode.

"You shouldn't be trying to think. I rang for the nurse and she should be here in a minute. She will give you something for the pain."

"Got to think—please no pain meds."

The door quietly opened and a white-clad nurse walked briskly into the room; a hypodermic needle in her hand.

"Now Mr. Miller, you won't say no to my little bitty shot will you. The doctor wants you to rest and not get agitated. You can think later, you are only making yourself worse." The nurse swiftly pushed the syringe into his arm and watched as Henry fought unconsciousness for a moment, and then slowly closed his eyes.

"He should sleep for awhile now and will feel much better when he wakes up the next time," the nurse said.

"He will be okay, won't he?" Roberta asked.

"Of course he will; now don't you worry." The nurse finished taking his vitals and briskly walked to the door. "Call me if he wakes again."

"All right." Roberta turned back to the young man who had become very important to her for some reason.

Henry opened his eyes again. He tested his pain level and decided; maybe he might live after all. One other thing occurred to him; for one he needed to use the bathroom and for another he wanted to get out of this bed before that nurse gave him another shot.

"Oh, Henry, you're awake. Albert, Henry's awake," Mrs. Miller said excitedly.

"I told you he would be all right, now just cool it and let the boy alone," Mr. Miller said as he patted his son's arm. "You gave us a scare, boy."

"Sorry," Henry crocked. "Need a drink and the bathroom."

"Martha, give the boy a sip of water," Mr. Miller said. "You can go get the nurse and I'll help the boy to the bathroom."

"Do you think you should let him get up without the nurse here?"

"He won't want the nurse to help him to the bathroom. Now you run along. We'll be fine."

Mrs. Miller got to her feet and gave Henry's hand a squeeze. "I won't be long. Albert, you be careful and don't let him fall."

"I won't, Mama."

Henry smiled as he watched the big man pulled the covers back so Henry could sit up. "Thanks, you're right, I don't want the nurse in here when I go to the bathroom." He pushed up and stopped for a minute.

"You okay?"

"Yeah, I need to wait until my head stops going in circles. Boy does it ever hurt, but don't tell the nurse that. I don't want another pain shot."

It wasn't long until Henry was back in the bed and as he lay down he gave a huge sigh. "I guess I'm not as strong as I thought. Where's Roberta?"

"Her dad came and got her. He said she had a pile of work to get through. She said she would be back after five. You know Eddy is going to throw a fit when he finds out you two are dating."

"He'll have to get over it. He's the one that broke it off."

"I didn't know that. When did he do that?"

"Just before he headed to Grandmas; over the phone if you can believe that."

"Good grief."

The soft sound of the door opening broke in on the two men's conversation. Mrs. Miller and a white clad nurse came into the room.

"How is our patient doing?" the cheerful voice of the nurse asked.

"I've been better, but my head doesn't hurt as much as it did, so don't give me another shot, please."

"I'll wait until Dr. Russell makes his rounds and let him decide whether you should have another shot or not. I take it you were able to make it to the bathroom all right."

"Yes, with my dad's help."

"Good, I know you probably didn't want to use a bedpan."

"Huh, no, I can get up with help."

A short tap sounded on the door and Sheriff Young came in carrying his Stetson. "Am I interrupting anything?"

"No, Sheriff, I was just checking on my patient."

"Can I ask him a few questions?"

"If you keep it short, let me know when you leave."

"I'll do that, thank you, ma'am."

The nurse bustled out.

"You don't want us in here, do you?" Mr. Miller asked.

"Why don't you take the little lady down and get her a cold drink. I won't be long," Sheriff Young said.

"But—but," Mrs. Miller said.

"Come along, Mother, this is police business and he won't hurt your wee lamb."

"Oh, Albert, really," Mrs. Miller said as she followed her husband out of the room.

"How you feeling?"

"I've felt better. My head still feels like it weights a ton, and I try not to move it if I can help it."

"You're lucky; doc says that if your assailant had hit you just a little bit harder, you would be at a funeral home not at the hospital."

"That's a cheerful thought."

"Just bear that in mind. What do you remember about yesterday?"

"Not much. I think I had made an appointment with Phillip Johnson to ask him about his father, but I'm not even sure about that."

"Why did you want to talk with Phillip Johnson?"

"Ole Matt at the marina mentioned that he and Walter Whitney had been a team on that pyramid scam that ended in Whitney going to jail. That and the fact that I had run into Phillip on Labor Day made me wonder if his dad had come back to town."

"You told me about Matt, and I think you mentioned seeing Phillip on the lake road, but why do you think Luther Johnson may be back in town?"

"I don't know, just a hunch. I'm not even sure about my reasoning. It hurts too much to think right now."

"Well, you and that little Hamilton gal cool it, will you? Let the experts do their job. If you remember anything else you give me a call and I'll take care of it."

"Okay, I will. I sure don't want to get hit over the head again, that's for sure."

Sheriff Young got up from his chair and put his hat back on. "I'll check in on you tomorrow to see if you remember anything else."

"Thanks." Henry watched as the sheriff walked out the door. He closed his eyes for a minute and tried to remember more about what he had done the day before. He remembered calling Phillip's house. He had talked with Phillip's mother and she had told him that Phillip was working on a construction job for Summers Construction. What had he done then? There seemed to be spots of his memory that were blank. He reached up to run his fingers through his hair and hit the bandage on his head. Good grief, that hurt, he thought. Maybe he did need to sleep some more. Maybe it would help his memory if he just closed his eyes and let sleep overtake him.

The next time Henry awoke, Roberta was sitting by the side of the bed. He gave her a slight smile and reached out to take her hand. "Hi."

"Hi, yourself, how are you feeling?"

"Better I think. Since you're here I take it that it is after five."

"Yep, actually it is five-thirty. You've been sleeping for a while, your mom said. They have gone home."

"I'm glad. I know staying here watching me sleep can't be all that exciting."

"You'd be surprised. I brought a book, so I've been reading. Do you remember anymore?"

"A little, I wonder what Phillip thought when we didn't show up last night. I had a hard time convincing him to even meet with us."

"Maybe you should call him tonight and set up another time."

"The sheriff asked us to leave it alone, and maybe we should. I don't want you to get hurt and I certainly don't want to get hit on the head again."

"But-but, okay." Roberta sighed. "Dad pretty much said the same thing. He was not real pleased when he found out where we were going. I just hate to drop it completely."

"I know, I feel the same way. I think I will call him to explain. Where are my clothes?"

"In the closet I think; unless your mom took them home."

"Will you check and if my clothes are still there check my shirt pocket. There should be a piece of paper with a phone number."

Roberta checked the closet and came back to the bed with a piece of paper clutched in her hand. "Is this it?" She handed Henry the paper.

"Yes, will you dial that number for me?"

Roberta took the piece of paper and laid it by the telephone. She dialed the number and waited until it started to ring before she handed the receiver to Henry.

"Hello, Phillip? This is Henry Miller."

"What happened, you never showed."

"Sorry about that. I ended up in the hospital with a concussion."

"Really, did you have a wreck?"

"Nah, wish it was something like that. Someone hit me on the head."

"What? Good grief man, why would anyone do that?"

"I'm not sure, but I think it may have been because I started asking questions about Walter Whitney and your dad."

"My dad, why would anyone care if you asked questions about him?"

"I'm not sure. I was hoping you could tell me where he is and if you know if he had anything to do with Walter Whitney after he got out of jail."

"Who is this Whitney you keep talking about? I've never heard of him."

"I was told your dad knew Whitney before he was sent to prison."

"So, what if he had known him?"

"Whitney was found murdered out at the lake on Labor Day."

"And you think my dad had something to do with that?"

"I don't know what to think. I was hoping I could talk with your dad and find out more about what is going on."

Silence extended for a couple of minutes and Henry was afraid Phillip had hung up.

"You knew my dad has just gotten out of prison?"

"I wasn't for sure, but I knew it was possible."

"I went to see him on Labor Day. I hadn't seen him in ten years. He was camping out in an old derelict house near where you saw me. I believed all his lies. I even found him a job where I went to work. He never showed up that first day, nor has he been there since."

"Have you seen him or talked with him since Labor Day?"

"Oh, yeah, I went to see him when he didn't show up that first day to see why he hadn't shown up. He couldn't go to work because he was drunk. I got so angry; I ended up calling him everything but a white man, and stormed out of the house. I haven't seen or heard from him since."

"So you haven't you seen him since then?"

"No, and I don't want to see him again. I should have listened to my Mom. She told me what he was like, but you know, he's my dad."

"I get you. Would you mind going out where he was staying and see if he's still there?"

"Sure, but you do understand I don't think my dad would have anything to do with killing that Whitney you mentioned. My dad may be a lot of things, but he isn't a murderer."

"I sure hope he isn't. That isn't something anyone wants to believe about their dad."

"Where can I get a hold of you?"

"I'm at Campbell Memorial right now." Henry looked at Roberta and she handed Henry a piece of paper with the phone number written on it. He gave Phillip the number. "Just let me know won't you?"

"Sure. I'll run out there right now. I'm kind of curious about him, and I've felt bad about the argument we had. I'll call you as soon as I get back to the house."

"Sounds good, I'll be waiting for your call."

Henry handed the receiver back to Roberta and she hung it up. "So he doesn't know if his dad is even still in town?"

"That's the way it sounds. When you hear stories like that it makes you more thankful than ever for the parents you have."

"You can say that again."

Chapter 14

Phillip Johnson slowly hung up the telephone and stood staring down at the instrument sitting on the kitchen counter. He didn't know what to think about Henry Miller sticking his nose into the Johnson's family business. Phillip strode over to the coffee pot on the stove and poured himself a cup of coffee. As he took a sip he wrinkled his nose, and reached over and turned off the burner. That coffee had definitely been on the fire too long. Pouring the coffee down the drain, and setting the cup in the sink, he wandered out into the living room.

What was he going to do about Henry's request? Flinging himself down in the overstuffed chair, he laid his head against the back and closed his eyes. He mulled over his conversation with Henry. On the one hand he would like to know where his dad was and that he was alright, but on the other he really didn't want to see him again. Life had suddenly become very complicated. Because of the carpet, he didn't hear his little sister walk into the room.

"Who was on the phone just now?" Tammy asked. She pulled a strand of her dark brown hair forward and twisted it around her finger. "I am expecting a call, so I was hoping it was for me."

"It was a friend of mine," Phillip mumbled without looking at Tammy.

"Oh, I hoped it was for me."

"If it had been for you I would have called you. If you must know it was Henry Miller."

"I don't know him, do I?" Tammy dropped down on the couch losing interest. "I'm expecting a call from a girlfriend; I hoped it was her."

"Sorry, it wasn't. How is school going?" Phillip opened his eyes and looked over at his sister. She was going to be a real beauty when she matured a little more. Her dark brown hair that she mostly wore in a pony tail, and her dark brown eyes that seemed too big for her elfin face really made her stand out. He wondered if he should be paying more attention to her activities. He was the head of the family now, more or less. He knew now for sure that his dad would never be back or even care a rip for any of them.

"Oh…you know, its okay, I guess. Mary Wilson moved during the summer so I have no one to hang with. I really hate it because we have been best friends since the first grade. I really miss her."

"You'll find a new best friend. Sometimes it better if we don't get too close to another person."

"Speak for yourself, I like having friends to hang with. You may not, but I do."

"I guess girls are different."

"Was your phone call not from a friend?" Tammy asked with a frown.

"We're not friends exactly; more like acquaintances. He is a guy I knew in school, but we didn't run around together. He hung out with a whole different group than I did."

"You know Mom didn't like the guys you hung out with. She was afraid you would get into trouble, and she was right."

"I learned my lesson. Six months in juvie made a believer out of me. I realized I never wanted to go to a real jail. Being locked up was for the birds. So you stay away from people that might get you in trouble."

"I will," Tammy said.

"I'm glad to hear you say you learned your lesson," Sophia Johnson said as she walked into the room. She had on her waitress uniform and she dug through her purse with a frown on her face.

"Have you seen my keys?"

"Are you leaving for work already?" Tammy asked.

"You know I have to work, so yes, I'm leaving for work. Have you started your homework yet?"

"I will after I eat. Did you leave us something for supper?"

"Of course, it's in the oven as usual. Phillip, how's the new job?"

"It's okay, I'm learning fast and Mr. Summers seemed pleased with my performance so far."

"See that you keep it that way. We need your extra income."

"I know, and I intend to continue working. I just wish I had been able to go to college instead of screwing up like I did."

"I'm not sure college is for the likes of us. Mother always called us poor white trash," Sophia said.

"We are not!" Tammy said indignantly. "How can you say that? Why would Grandma say something like that?"

"I guess because of your father," Sophia said. "You know they didn't get along."

"She never did have a good word to say about him did she?" Phillip asked.

"She didn't. There really wasn't much good to say about him." Sophia looked over at her son who was the spitting image of the man she had married. At eighteen, and pregnant, she hadn't had much choice. Her dad threatened to kill Luther and throw her out of the house. Luther, at twenty, really didn't want the responsibility of a family, but neither did he want her dad to shoot him. He hung in there until after Phillip was born, but after that he would disappear for long periods of time, and she never knew where he was or who he was with. He came back one time long enough to get her pregnant with Tammy, and left again. She brushed away a stray tear, and chastised herself for still caring.

"Mom, have you heard from Dad?" Phillip asked.

"Why would I have heard from your father? He and I are divorced. When he disappeared ten years ago, I decided I never wanted to see him again."

"You know he's back in town. I just thought maybe he may have gotten in touch with you."

"Daddy was in town and no one bothered to let me know?" Tammy said angrily.

"The less contact you have with your father the better off you are," Sophia said. "I've got to go. I'll check up on you before bed time. Tammy be sure you're in bed by ten, hear."

"Of course, Mom," Tammy said wrinkling her nose. "You know I always get in bed by ten. Besides since Mary moved, I don't have anyone to talk with on the phone."

"I know you felt bad about Mary leaving, but that's life. You might as well get used to it," Sophia said. "Ah, here are my keys. I've got to run, y'all be good, you hear."

The two siblings watched their mother hurry out of the room. Tammy turned to look at Phillip. "Was it just me, or did Mom sidestep your question about Dad?"

"I didn't notice, but now that you mention it, she didn't say she hadn't heard from him. Do you think she has seen him?"

"Who am I to say? Y'all didn't even tell me that he was around."

"Sorry, kid, he contacted me, but he asked me not to say anything. I thought he intended to settle down this time. He talked that way. He even talked about getting a job. You do know he just got out of the slammer."

"Maybe Grandma was right; maybe we are just poor white trash." Tears welled up in Tammy's eyes.

"Hey, don't cry. Grandma didn't know what she was talking about. Her definition of poor white trash and mine are different, and I don't think we are."

"But Daddy is a criminal, and you've been to juvenile detention; what else makes you poor white trash than that?"

"Poor ways; you know derelict cars in the yard, trash spread over the place; that type of stuff makes you trashy."

"Thank goodness we aren't trashy in that manner. Let's go see what's in the oven, I'm hungry."

Just as they got into the kitchen, the phone rang. Tammy made a dive for the receiver and breathlessly said hello. "Oh, yes, he's here, can I say who's calling?" Tammy turned around and wrinkled her nose. "It's for you. Don't talk too long."

Phillip took the receiver and grinned at his sister. "Hello, who is this?"

"The name is Matt-I'm an old friend of your dad's."

"Matt—Matt who?"

"Matt Walsh. You may not have heard about me, it may have been before your time."

"I vaguely remember a Matt. What can I do for you?"

"I was wondering if you have spoken with your dad lately."

"Why?"

"I was just wondering. No skin off of my nose if he hasn't gotten in touch with you since he got out of jail."

"Although it's none of your business, I have spoken with him, and before you ask, I don't have a clue where he is now."

"Well, dang, I was hoping I could talk with him. He and I have a lot of catching up to do. I haven't seen him in a month of Sundays. He tell you where he was heading?"

"No, he didn't. Really, what's all this about?"

"Nothing just thought maybe you knew his whereabouts. I'll keep checking. I really wanted to talk with him."

"No point in calling back here, I don't look for him to show up anytime soon."

"You never know. See you around."

Phillip stood staring into space with a frown on his face.

"Who was that?" Tammy asked.

"Someone asking about Dad, what bothers me is why all of a sudden so many people are asking about him."

"You would think after all this time no one would be interested in him. How long has he been in town, do you know?"

"Not really. I talked with him on Labor Day, and I haven't seen him since."

"Phillip, do you think he has gotten himself in trouble?"

"I don't know what to think, and it has me scared to death for him and for us."

"What do you mean? We don't even know where he is, how could we be in trouble?"

"We may not know where he is, but do the people looking for him realize that we don't? There are just too many people looking for him."

Tammy rubbed her hands up and down on her arms. "You're scaring me."

"I think we need to be scared. Dad may know that people are after him, and that may be why he has disappeared."

"You think he is trying to protect us?"

"I'm not sure he cares about us one way or the other, but he does care about his own skin and if he knows people are looking for him, he will want to hide out somewhere. That acquaintance of mine that I spoke with earlier is looking for him too."

"What's he done?" Tammy cried out, and tears began to roll down her cheeks.

"I don't know. I wish I knew, but I just don't know."

A ragged man hunkered down in a drainage ditch and watched three men dig a hole and then bury a dead body. He had never been so scared in his life. Not knowing why, he felt the body could have been his. He left the security of the tumbled down shack he had been living in right after he had seen his son, and began to rough it out in the open. He saw now he shouldn't have left the shack, except his intuition warned him that it wasn't safe anymore. When he left prison he came back to see his kids and his ex-wife, but she made it plain she didn't want anything to do with him. He managed to talk her into giving him some money, and she even gave him some food from that café she worked at, the problem was that had been a day ago and he was hungry again. He didn't dare go to a café or any place like that because someone was sure to notice him. He really intended to settle down this time, he even told his son that he would get a real job and work for a change. But when he saw the Sheriff and his deputies supervise the removal of a body, it really spooked him. Now there was another body. He wanted to high-tail it then, but he was dead broke. That was why he had taken the chance on contacting his ex.

  He watched the little gal drive away in the car; he was sure those men had obviously not intended for her to leave. He didn't recognize her, but then again he didn't recognize the three men either. At one time, he knew just about everyone in Parker County. If he didn't know them he had seen them somewhere, but now there were just too many new people around. Ten years did make a difference.

  He had been looking for another good place to spend the night when he had heard the gun shot.

Curiosity had led him to this abandoned house. The pickup parked in front of the house sparked his interest. He needed just such a vehicle to get out of the county. Then the car, the girl drove off in, pulled up next to the pickup and two men got out with what looked like food. His interest really did heighten then; so he waited for a little while, intending to get in one of the vehicles and drive away. He figured these guys were crooks so they wouldn't go to the police about the stolen car.

It stunned him when he saw who came out of the house and got into the pickup. Ten years could really make a difference in the looks of someone, but he would have recognized him anywhere. He was ten years older and a little pudgy around the middle, but it was still that no good so and so who turned him into the police. Luther always suspected he wanted to move in on Sophie, but according to his son; Sophie had never remarried.

Still holding back, he waited to see if anyone came out to the car. When no one did, he stood up and started edging toward the vehicle; that was when the three men came outside. He hunkered back down and waited some more. He was just getting his nerve back when the front door slammed open and the little gal ran outside and headed for the vehicle; his vehicle, damn it! She jumped into the car and started it up and was headed out of the yard when the three men came running from the back.

He slumped back down and closed his eyes. There just had to be a way out of here; there just had to be. Turning his back to the big oak he was hiding behind, he rubbed his face. All was quiet for some time when a shout startled him. Peering around the tree, he watched as the men went into the house and came back out carrying the body around back and placed it in the hole they had dug. Once they covered the hole, they left not only the grave but the house as well. He watched until they disappeared from sight. Could this be his lucky day after all, he wondered. He might accidently be able to spend the night inside, and maybe there would be a bed. All he had to worry about was the guy in the pickup. If he came back, Luther knew he would be done for, because he knew the man well enough to know he would shoot him on sight, no questions or explanations, he would be dead.

Chapter 15

Linda drove as fast as she dared down the winding road. Sobs racked her body and tears streamed down her face. She had gotten away, but where was she? It appeared to be a desolate countryside. Live oaks and scrub brush on either side of her and no one in sight. At least she didn't have to worry about the men she left behind. They were on foot at least for the time being. She should head to the nearest police department, but she had no idea where the nearest one was. The dirt road she traveled came to an abrupt halt at a small asphalt road that headed toward her right. There was a fence to her left and a danger sign in the middle of it. All she could do was follow the road and see where she came out.

    A few minutes later she saw a turn-out so she turned into it and sat looking around. It was so very quiet, not even any bird songs filled the air. She took a deep breath, wiping her face with the tail of her shirt; she glanced over at the sack she had snatched up as she left the house. Opening it with care she spied a sandwich wrapped in wax paper. Food, she thought, she unwrapped the sandwich and took a big bite. Ah, she thought, ham and cheese, her very favorite. Of course anything would be her favorite right now. She wished she had grabbed a drink as she fled the scene of her kidnapping, but she had been in too much of a hurry. Finishing the sandwich, she looked in the sack again and brought up a sack of chips. She laid it aside for later.

Putting the car in reverse, she got back on the road again, if not like new, at least in a little better shape than she had been before she had escaped. The road she was driving down finally dead-ended into a bigger asphalt road, this one went both ways. She stopped and looked up and down trying to decide which way she should go, neither way looked promising so she did the old eenie meenie miney mo rhyme and chose the one the rhyme ended on which was to the right. She glanced to her right and realized she was near a lake, but which lake she hadn't a clue. She wished she knew where the men took them? The men had put bags over their heads so they could not tell where they were being taken. Walter thought they might be going east toward Dallas, but if that was the case wouldn't there be more people around;

all she could see was empty waste land. Linda shook her head to clear it and found that she was coming to another road. She turned down it and it seemed to go on forever, but it suddenly stopped at a four lane highway. There was a cemetery on her left and a sign that said turn left for Fort Worth. Should she go back to Fort Worth or should she head west? So she did the rhyme once more and turned west.

  Linda continued to second guess herself as she drove down Highway 80 toward Weatherford. Weatherford was where Walter intended to go the next day; maybe Walter got away and would find him there. Anything was better than thinking he might be dead. She pulled up to the first traffic light on what appeared to be the center of town. A courthouse sat in the middle of the square and Highway 80 went around both sides of the courthouse. It was a beautiful old courthouse made out of white brick; four sided like most of the courthouses in Texas, there was a red roof with a clock in the tower. Of course the clock didn't work like most of the old clocks.

  Okay, she thought, here was the courthouse so where was the police station? She hadn't seen anything that would tell her. She drove through the square and two blocks away on her left she spotted the City Hall. Surely the police station was close by. She turned down by the City Hall building and sure enough there was the Police Station. Taking a deep breath, she turned into the parking lot and still shaking all over she headed inside.

 Henry turned restlessly in the hospital bed trying to find a comfortable spot. He sure hoped the doctor let him go home tomorrow. He was all alone, his parents left about seven and Roberta left about eight, since then he had done nothing but think and twist and turn in the bed. The thinking got him nowhere at all; he hadn't been able to come up with a single reason why someone would want to hit him on the head. Henry checked the clock and groaned. It was only a quarter to ten; it was going to be a very long night.

 The shrill ringing of the telephone made him jump. Who in the world could be calling him at this hour, he wondered, as he fumbled for the receiver. He hoped it was Roberta calling to tell him goodnight. The more he saw of her the more she became important to him. He hoped against hope that she felt the same way.

"Hello."

"Henry Miller, is this you?"

"Yes, who is this?" Henry reached down and moved the head of his bed up.

"It's Matt, sorry to bother you this late at night. I've been looking for you all day. Figured you would be at the marina, but you never showed up."

"Couldn't make it today, are the fish biting?"

"Nah, still too hot, I guess. What I called about is to see if you have been able to get a hold of Luther Johnson?"

Henry stopped what he had been about to say and closed his eyes for a minute. A trickle of fear ran up and down his spine. He wasn't sure why, but something seemed off about Matt asking him about Luther, especially this late at night. He couldn't remember what he even told him to make him think he was interested in Luther. Darn this knock on his head. "As a matter of fact, I'm not any closer to finding him now than I was the last time I talked with you. Have you heard from him?"

"I doubt he would contact me, you know I told you that he and I had a falling out 'cause I wouldn't buy into his pyramid scheme. I hoped you knew something. If you do find him, would you let me know? I want to see him and tell him that I have no hard feelings anymore."

"Sure, sounds good. I'll do that."

"Where are you anyway? I called your house and your dad gave me this number to reach you."

"I'm in the hospital. Someone tried to find out just how hard my head is."

"You don't say, weird world we're living in, ain't it? You're okay aren't you?"

"Oh, yes, I hope to go home tomorrow. I'm surprised Dad didn't tell you where I am."

"Well, you know, I think I got him out of bed. I felt real bad about calling so late. I didn't realize how late it was until he answered the phone. I won't keep you; I was just curious about Luther."

"Not a problem. I'll talk with you later." Henry hung up the receiver and lay staring up at the ceiling. He began to wonder just how good a friend Matt really had been to Luther. And why call this late at night. It didn't make a lot of sense. What had really happened all those years ago, he wondered. Something told him there was something rotten in Denmark. He wondered if the Sheriff had access to the court records of Whitney and Johnson. He needed to make a note or try to remember to ask Sheriff Young. It was surprising that Sheriff Young hadn't come back to talk with him. Henry lowered the bed and twisted trying to find a comfortable place, 'darn hospital bed,' he thought. He ended up on his back with his hands behind his head. Sheriff Young would probably come in the morning; maybe even before he went to work. Somewhere in those muddled thoughts Henry drifted off to sleep.

Just as he had thought Sheriff Young came into Henry's room around seven-thirty. The sheriff strode in with a frown on his face and carrying his hat. His boots clomping on the floor gave Henry plenty of warning that he had a visitor. He figured it had to be the sheriff; his dad's shoes didn't make that much noise.

"How you doing this morning," Sheriff Young growled. He pitched his hat on the night stand and sank wearily into the side chair.

"Better. I got a good night's sleep and I'm hoping the doctor will let me go home today. You don't look so good; have a bad night?"

"Was up early, bad wreck on 51, people will drive like a bat out of hell on that road."

"Sorry to hear that. Was there any deaths?"

"Probably will be, brought both drivers in here in critical condition." Sheriff Young sat staring into space and shook his head.

"Well, back to you, do you remember anymore than you did yesterday?"

"I'm not sure. I remember hearing a car door slam and footsteps headed my way. I didn't turn around to see who it was, I don't think. The next thing I remember was waking up here. Not much help, am I?"

"Didn't expect you to remember much more than that, no reason you should have turned to see who was headed your way. I'm sure it has to do with that murder case I'm working on, that is unless you made some boyfriend mad as a hatter because you stole his gal."

"I'm not much of a Casanova. Haven't stole anyone's gal lately; well, except for my brother's and he had already cut her lose."

"You talking about the Hamilton girl?"

"Yes, she had been dating my brother for awhile, but he broke it off."

"So we're back to the murder case. What you been stirring up now?"

"Nothing really, Roberta and I were going to meet Phillip Johnson and see if he would tell us about his dad's involvement with the murder victim. Of course we weren't even sure he was aware of his dad's involvement with Whitney."

"I got curious about that old case and pulled the records. Whitney swore the gun belonged to the murder victim and he had acted in self-defense. The problem was there were no other witnesses." Sheriff Young shook his head. "Hard to prove if there isn't any other witnesses and one of the men in question is dead."

"Luther Johnson wasn't involved in the trial?"

"No mention of him at all. Not even as a witness for the prosecution. I thought it a little strange myself, so I called up the District Attorney and had a chat with him. Problem is, he wasn't the D. A. then and couldn't tell me much. He promised to have one of his girls look up the file and get back to me."

"I had a weird phone call last night from old Matt Walsh."

"What in the world, what did he want?"

"He wanted to know if I had found Luther. He claimed he and Luther had a falling out because of the pyramid scheme Luther and Whitney were selling and he wanted to make nice. I get the feeling that more is going on than we are aware of."

"You may have hit the nail on the head. Matt Walsh...Hum," Sheriff Young said shaking his head. "Never heard of him getting into any kind of trouble and I don't think I noticed his name in the court records I read."

"He claimed he never bought into the scheme. I don't know what it is exactly, but something doesn't ring true in all of this. I haven't known him long, I met him at the marina and he and I have fished together some. He seems harmless enough."

"I always thought he was harmless, but if I've learned anything in the law enforcement field, no one is completely harmless. Sometimes it's money or greed, sometimes it's a mental sickness, sometimes it's vengeance, and sometimes it's just plain meanness."

"I did call Phillip yesterday afternoon late and spoke with him. He said he had seen his father on Labor Day, but hadn't seen him since. I'm not sure I believe him, but that is what he said."

"No reason he should lie. Did he tell you where he saw him?"

"An old run down shack on the east side of the lake, is what he said. I know about where I saw him on Labor Day so the shack should be easy to find."

"There are several old homesteads east of the lake; could be any of them. I'll have Fisk check them out." Sheriff Young stood up and reached for his hat. "I won't stay any longer. You take it easy and stay out of this. I know it's hard, but after your run in with whatever you were hit with I think you should cool it."

"I think you're right. So long and you take it easy."

Chapter 16

The police officer listened to Linda as she poured out her story. Sometimes he would stop her and ask her to repeat something, but mostly he just listened. When she finished, he shook his head. "Miss, you are very lucky to have gotten out of there alive. I'm surprised they didn't shoot you as you were fleeing the scene." The policeman shook his head and made some more notes on the pad where he had written down her story.

"I hadn't thought of that. I guess I was so frightened I never thought of the consequences of my escape. I just knew I wanted, no needed, to get away. I would have run all the way here if I had to; thank goodness I didn't."

"Tell me your name again I didn't write it down."

"Linda Kay Warner. Please help me. I don't know what to do or where to go. All of my things and my husband's things are in a hotel in Fort Worth."

"Now don't you worry, Mrs. Warner, I'm sure we can get an officer with the Fort Worth Police

Department to go to your hotel room and gather up your belongings."

"Oh, yes, please, I don't want to go back there. I'm afraid that those men will come looking for me again."

"Is there anyone you would like to call?"

"Can I? It would be long distance. I'm from Huntsville."

The officer turned the instrument toward her. "You just go ahead and call, but keep it short."

"Thank you." Linda picked up the receiver and with shaking hands, she dialed her pastor's number.

"Hello, Reverend Joe Hardy speaking, how may I help you?"

"Brother Joe, this is Linda Warner."

"Linda, how are you. I have been so worried. Where are you?"

"Oh Brother Joe…" That was all Linda got out before she broke down and started sobbing. The police officer watched her for a moment, and then gently removed the receiver from her hand.

"Hello, Brother Joe, this is Officer Simmons with the Weatherford, Texas Police Department. Mrs. Warner isn't able to talk right now. She wanted to call someone from home and I guess she picked you."

"Is she all right, and by the way, her name is Mrs. Whitney not Warner?"

"She told me her name was Linda Kay Warner."

"That's her maiden name. She married Walter Whitney a little over a month ago. I understand from a Miss Hamilton, with Hamilton Investigations there in your town, that Walter is dead; is that true and does Linda know that?"

"No, sir, not as far as I can tell; she assumes he is. I'll have to admit that her story was a little incoherent, but she did say she didn't really know what happened to him."

"You do know a Miss Hamilton, don't you?"

"Not personally, no sir, but I know who you're talking about. Her father has been a Private Investigator here for a number of years."

"Good, I got to worrying, after I spoke with her, that I might have been talking with Linda's kidnappers."

"No, sir, Mr. Hamilton isn't one of the bad guys. She's calmed down a bit, so I'll put her back on the phone." The young officer handed Linda the receiver.

"Sorry, Brother Joe, I just broke down. It's too long a story to tell you over the phone. I'll try to call you later and tell you all about what has happened. I just needed to hear a familiar voice, and Brother Joe, would you pray for Walter and me?"

"Of course I will, but Linda, I understand that Walter is gone."

"I know he's gone."

"I don't mean just gone away, but gone like he is with the Lord now."

"No-no, he can't be. How do you know that? Don't say that. Oh, please, don't say he's dead."

"That's what I was told. I'm sorry. Do you need money to get home?"

"Money, no—I don't know. Just pray for us, please."

There was silence over the phone line and then with a sigh Brother Joe began to pray. "Our most precious heavenly Father, look after your child, Linda and keep her safe. Calm her and give her peace. And dear Lord, you tell us that with your help nothing is impossible, so I'm asking you to protect your child and if Walter isn't dead bring him safely back to his loving wife. These things we ask in your son's Jesus' name, amen."

"Thank you so much Brother Joe. I feel calmer already. I'll call you again when I know more about what's going on."

"God go with you, child."

Linda slowly replaced the receiver on the telephone base and looked at the young officer with tears once more in her eyes. "Walter is dead, isn't he?"

"I think so ma'am."

"I knew it; deep in my heart I knew it. I didn't want to admit it, but I knew it. What will I do now? Where will I go?"

"Ma'am…"

"I'm sorry, I'm just thinking aloud. I'm so tired and hungry, and I don't have any money; what am I going to do?"

"Now don't you worry, as soon as one of the other officers gets back in I'll send them out to get you something to eat and in the meantime why don't I take you back to one of the jail cells, no one is in them right now, and you can rest there until the Chief gets back in."

Linda took a deep breath and smiled at the young officer. He blushed at her smile and got up to lead her to one of the empty cells so she could rest.

Several hours later Linda woke up in a panic. Wondering where she was, she sat up on the cot and looked around her. The bars startled her until she remembered that she was in a jail cell that the nice police officer had led her to. She needed to use the bathroom very badly and she was really hungry. She got up and headed toward the sound of voices. Suddenly, she stopped when she heard her name. Two male voices, she didn't recognize, were discussing her.

"When did Linda Whitney show up here?"

"According to the officer, she showed up around three in the afternoon. You were out of the office so he just left a message. I knew when he told me about her showing up that you would want to be the one to speak with her."

"I appreciate you letting me know. I have hit a dead end on this murder case, and I hope she will be able to help me out. I tell you what, there are just too many deaths happening in our county, and I'm getting too old."

"Yeah, I know what you mean. I have trouble with the City Council and I am sure you have equal trouble with the Commissioner's Court. They want maximum police coverage at minimum cost."

"Tell me about it. I ended up having Robert Hamilton do some leg work for me because my few officers are run off their legs."

"Robert's a good man. I've used him a few times myself."

"I figured he owed me since his girls are the ones that seem to be finding all the dead bodies around here." Sheriff Young said with a laugh. "Back to Mrs. Whitney, I don't want to wake her but I would really like to talk with her."

"I'll go back and check on her. Maybe she's awake by now."

Linda walked through the doorway and tried to smile at the two older men who were talking. "I'm awake, but I could sure use the bathroom before we do any lengthy talking."

"Mrs. Whitney," Chief of Police Wilbert Stanford stood up and shook her hand. "The bathroom is just down the hall on your left. If you'll come back in here when you're through, we would appreciate it."

"I won't be but a minute, and maybe some food?" Linda smiled at the balding Chief of Police.

She returned in a few minutes and smiled at the wrapped sandwich and glass of water that sat on the chief's desk. She sat down in front of the food and took a sip of water and unwrapped the sandwich.

"Okay, gentlemen, what do you wish to know?"

"Mrs. Whitney, I'm Sheriff Johnny Young, and I'm the one handling the murder of your husband. At least we assume the body we found is your husband. There was no ID on him, but the finger prints appear to match. We would like you to take a look and make a positive ID if you don't mind."

"I want to see the body, so I can prove to myself that he's really dead." Tears welled up in her eyes; she laid the half-eaten sandwich down and began to look for a tissue.

Sheriff Young handed her his handkerchief. "I would appreciate it. Now ma'am, tell me your story. I know you told the police officer and he has written up a report for me, but I would like to hear it from your own lips."

"Of course," Linda said, and she began to tell him what had happened from the time the men showed up at their hotel room until her escape.

"Do you think you can show me where you were being held?"

"I'm not sure. I was so frightened. I just followed the road and took whatever turn I came too. All I can say is that I can try."

"Did you know the men who held you captive?"

"No, and I don't think Walter did either. He knew they were a danger to us and he continued to reassure me after they brought us to the house they held us in, but to know them personally, neither he nor I did."

"Okay, so obviously they were just hired help. Did you hear them talking about why they had kidnapped you?"

"I heard one of the men say something about a stash of money, and that they hoped the boss would share with them if they found it for him."

"Money, well, now that is interesting." Sheriff Young turned to Chief Stanford. "You hear anything about there being a stash of money hidden or not having showed up when Whitney got arrested?"

"They got him in Fort Worth, so I wasn't too involved in the case. I was just a police officer when this all went down. I don't remember anything being said about missing money around the office here. I think if there had been, the rumor mill would have been active."

"Nothing was said in the court trial about any money. I read the whole file, interesting, very interesting. Did Whitney say anything to you about him having money stashed somewhere?"

"No, we were sort of living on my money. I have a good job, or rather I had a good job, with a construction firm in Huntsville and so we were using my money. I'm afraid I never asked Walter if he had access to any money, I guess I just assumed he didn't."

"You know, Sheriff Young, it's possible that Whitney had the money he swindled out of people on that stock investment scam he ran and it could still be sitting in a bank somewhere," Chief Stanford said.

"It's possible, of course anything is possible. It could be that the man who hired those thugs just told them about some money being stashed away to make them eager to work for him," Sheriff Young mused. "It would definitely be interesting to talk with Luther Johnson. He may be the only one who would know if there was any money stashed away."

"Wait a minute, who did you just mention?" Linda asked.

"Luther Johnson, did Whitney ever mention him?" The sheriff asked.

"Just before Walter was released he asked me to do a couple of things for him."

"What were they?" Sheriff Young asked.

"He wanted me to find out where a couple of men went after they were released from prison. One was Kenny Wright, his cell mate and the other was Luther Johnson. He never told me why he wanted to know where they were even though I asked him several times. That is one of the reasons we came up here. They both had headed to Dallas. I begged him to forget about them; after all they were his past and I was his future. For some reason, he wouldn't let it go," Linda said as tears once more ran down her cheeks.

"You know its possible Luther knows where all that money is," Chief Stanford said.

"That's very possible. Why did he want to find Kenny Wright, do you know?"

"Not really. When we got to Fort Worth, he made a phone call; he wouldn't tell me who he was talking with, but I know he was very angry when he got off the phone with whoever he spoke with."

"Hum—it would be interesting to find this Kenny Wright. I'll put Kathleen Hamilton on trying to trace him. If he's in Fort Worth the Tarrant County Sheriff might be able to help me," Sheriff Young said as he stood up. He turned back to Linda. "By the way do you know or did Whitney mention a woman by the name of Lana Jacob?"

"Lana Jacob—no—I don't—wait a minute, not a Lana Jacob, but—well, I did hear part of his conversation before he realized I was still in the room. He said something about not being a contractor and that Miss Jacob could look elsewhere for her contact. I thought it was a really strange terminology, but I had learned by then not to ask too many questions."

"Interesting, Mrs. Whitney, you have been an enormous help to me. Do you have a place to put up for tonight?"

"No, I have no money or ID; I'm not sure what I'll do."

"Don't you worry, I called my mother, she has a spare room and she's agreed to let you stay there until we get this all sorted," Chief Stanford said.

"Good, I'll know where to contact you if and when we find out more about what is going on. I'm going to asked Miss Hamilton to come get you tomorrow and take you to look at the body we have," Sheriff Young said.

Chief Sanger pushed a piece of paper over to Sheriff Young. "Here is Mom's address and phone number."

"Thanks, I will pass this on to the Hamilton's." He turned back toward Linda. "You take it easy and be very careful. I don't want to scare you, but I think someone wants to make sure you don't live through this; double check if anyone comes around and that includes Miss Hamilton."

Linda looked up at Sheriff Young and with an uncertain look on her face. "Why would anyone be interested in me? Walter told me I was just in the wrong place at the wrong time. I don't know anything about what's going on."

"It does sound as though Whitney tried to keep you ignorant of his activities, but we have a murder on our hands and it's possible that the murderer doesn't know how ignorant you are." Sheriff Young took a deep breath. "As I see it, it's possible you know more than you think you do; so you just be very careful."

Chapter 17

The full moon moved across a cloudless sky, giving a strange aspect to the colorless, silent arena to the area. The only light that could be seen was a flickering lantern in the old abandoned house. The figure of a man moved silently through the brush; letting the night and the shadows swallow his movement. He reached the house and peered through the window. He wasn't sure what he would see but the man he saw lounging on one of the beds in the front room took him by surprise. How had he gotten here and where were the three men and the lady captive? No one knew of this house; he had made sure of that. His parents had lived and died here. He had been born in the bed in the back room, he and his seven siblings. He had been the only one to survive, and now his worst enemy was lounging in his home. It had been his mother's dying wish that he keep the house and make it his home. A sneer curled his lips. He often wondered why his mother wanted him to keep this old dilapidated house. Even when he was young, it had been in bad repair. She had been frantic about it, clutching his hand with her arthritic one; begging him to never ever let the house go. Oh well, he thought that was a problem for another day. He knew what he had to do. He would never get a better chance to get rid of his enemy. It was what he lived for.

An hour later he returned carrying a container of gasoline. He had watched the house until the lantern had gone out, and then he went to a gas station and bought five gallons of gas. Now was his time. He moved silently through the brush back to the rear of the house. He didn't bother trying to see inside. There was nowhere else his enemy could have gone. His enemy would burn with the house; a fitting finish to a dubious friendship.

He splashed the gasoline in a stream around the house, finishing with a bigger stream on the front steps. There wasn't a proper porch; they had been too poor to have a proper porch; rage at their poverty still burned in him. The old steps would have to do. He reached in his pocket and pulled out a cigarette lighter; he flicked it once and watched as the flames started licking the fuel. A cruel smile curled his lips and he slowly turned and walked away. He was half way back to his vehicle, and the roar of the fire filled the air. He never heard the rattle because his mind was on the death of his enemy, but he felt the thud on his ankle and the pain that shot up his leg. He knew what had happened, and he knew he would not live much longer than his victim.

Sheriff Young opened the door and walked into Hamilton Investigation. He was early, a little before eight, so he hadn't been sure they would even be open yet, but the turn of the knob gave him assurance that someone was here. He had wanted to get an early start and maybe take Mrs. Whitney out toward Weatherford Lake to see if anything rang a bell with her. Old abandoned homesteads were numerous out toward the lake; that and the water shed were two of the reasons the lake had been built out there. West Texas wasn't noted for its heavy rain fall so every little thing helped to bring water into a lake. The City Council had known it needed to build the lake sooner or later before the growth of the city overcame their source of water. The few water wells and Sunshine Lake out north of town wouldn't be enough before too long. He smiled and shook his head; for once the City Council had made a wise decision.

"Hello, anyone working today?" Sheriff Young called.

Roberta came into the reception area carrying a mug of coffee. "Sheriff Young, good morning, good to see you. What can I do for you?"

"I wanted to see if you or your sister would do me a favor this morning," Sheriff Young said as he sat down and laid his hat on the reception desk.

"I will if I can, what do you want?" Roberta asked as she sat down behind the desk.

"Where's that sister of yours? Shouldn't she be here?"

"She's over at the County Clerk's office. She'll be in later."

"I wanted one of you to do me a favor. When do you expect her in?"

"I'm not sure. What did you need us for, can I help?"

"I'm not sure; your dad may not want you involved."

"It's owing to what it's for, is this concerning the Whitney Case?"

"In a way, Mrs. Whitney turned up at the city police station yesterday afternoon and I need her to make a positive ID on our murder victim."

"Did she really? That's wonderful. Where had she been, do you know? Wait a minute I thought you knew for sure who the victim was."

"I do, or at least I think I do, but a positive ID from the spouse will reassure me. Mrs. Whitney had been kidnapped along with her husband. She managed to escape. From what she told me, they were not a very professional group of kidnappers."

"What do you want Kathleen to do?"

"I had hoped she would go with me to pick Mrs. Whitney up; she is staying with the Chief's mother, and come with her when I take her in to ID the body. I thought it might make her feel better if she had a woman with her."

"Oh, I see, I don't know why I couldn't do as well as Kathleen. Things are kind of quiet this morning and Dad should be in shortly. So we can ask him if it is alright if I go instead of Kathleen."

"Well, I suppose you would do as well as your sister. I'll speak with your dad as soon as he comes in and let him know how much I would appreciate your help. I would take a deputy with me, but since I don't have a female one it would be kinda hard."

Roberta laughed. "When are you macho men going to allow us women to join law enforcement? This is the twentieth century after all."

"Not while I'm still sheriff we won't." Sheriff Young slapped his leg for emphasis.

Roberta laughed at him and they were still laughing when her father walked through the door.

"What's so funny?" Robert asked.

"Nothing," Roberta said as she wiped her eyes. "Sheriff Young wants to speak with you."

"Come into my office. Is there coffee?"

"Yes sir," Roberta said; getting up from her desk to get her father a cup of coffee. Before she could finish pouring the coffee her dad called her name.

"Roberta, I need you in here."

"I'm coming, Dad," she called as she headed to his office with his coffee in her hand. She sat it on his desk. "What do you need?"

"Sheriff Young wishes you to go with him when he takes Mrs. Whitney to identify her husband's body. Do you think you're up to that?"

"As long as I don't have to look at the body also, I wouldn't mind going."

"I thought as long as we were out; I'd see if Mrs. Whitney can take us back to where she was held captive. Is it all right for Miss Hamilton to go with us?"

"Hum…" Robert frowned as he thought over Sheriff Young's proposal. "I guess. You sure make it hard on me."

"I'll take care of her as if she were my own; more than that I can't say."

"All right then, if Roberta wishes to go with you she may."

The two left the offices and headed out to Sheriff Young's car. It didn't take long for the trio to go to the funeral home where Walter Whitney's body was being held pending burial. Linda all but collapsed at the sight of her husband lying in a casket. Roberta slipped an arm around her and walked her slowly out to the office of the funeral home. Assuring the funeral director that she would be back to arrange for the funeral, Linda followed the sheriff and Roberta back to his car.

"Sorry, to have to put you through that, ma'am," Sheriff Young said as he unlocked the car door for the girls.

"I appreciate you bringing a woman along with you," Linda said as she caught her breath in a sob. "I should go back in there and pay the funeral home and make arrangements for his burial."

"It's waited this long, it can wait another day or two. What I would like if you don't mind, is to see if we can locate where you were being held. It might tell us a lot."

"I told you, I'm not sure I can find it again."

"Do you mind trying?"

Wiping her eyes, Linda looked over at Sheriff Young and then glanced back at Roberta. "Can she go along, also?"

"I planned to, Mrs. Whitney. Sheriff Young won't harm you, but I can understand if you feel uncomfortable being alone with a strange man."

Linda took a deep breath and stared out of the windshield. "Okay, let's go. I'll do my best."

When the sheriff got to the first exit to Weatherford Lake he slowed down and Linda shook her head. "No, not here, I remember there was a cemetery by where I turned on to the highway."

"Okay, I know where you are talking about," Sheriff Young said as he continued down Highway 80.

"There, that's it, I turned on the highway from that road, but before that I just don't know."

"Didn't you say you made all right hand turns?"

"Yes, yes I did, but I'm not sure how many."

"We'll just have to play it by ear."

They drove for another thirty minutes when Linda grabbed Sheriff Young's arm. "There, see that road there, that's it, I'm-I'm pretty sure."

"Okay," Sheriff Young made the left hand turn and drove slowly down the rutted lane. He slowed to a stop when he saw a beat up pickup truck blocking the road. "Well, I'll be a monkey's uncle, what have we here?" He pulled the car up next to the pickup and stared at the truck.

"Yuk, what is that smell?" Roberta asked.

"Smells like something big has burned. That little spell of rain we had early this morning probably put it out. Good thing too, this whole countryside could have burned." Sheriff Young got out of the car and the women followed.

He stopped short and held out his arms. "What in the world?" He walked over to the body lying about fifty yards from the pickup.

"Who is it? Is he dead?" Roberta asked.

"Not sure," Sheriff Young said as he squatted down by the body. He gently turned the man over and felt for a pulse by his neck. "He's dead all right. Not sure what happened. I better get on my radio and call for Whites to send an ambulance." He gave a sigh and stood up shaking his head. "If it isn't one thing it's three."

"How did he die?" Roberta asked. "I don't see any blood."

"Don't know for sure, but the coroner will tell us."

"Do you recognize him?" Roberta asked looking at Linda.

Linda looked at her and then at the dead body. "I'm not sure. He's not one of the four men who held me captive, but there was a fifth one that I never saw. I just heard his voice."

The sheriff walked back to stand by the girls and stared down at the body. "Well, got that done, you girls can get back in the car now if you don't mind. Don't want to contaminate the crime scene."

"You think someone murdered him?" Roberta asked.

"Don't look like it but who knows. I'm going on up the road a ways and see what burned."

"I think if Linda doesn't mind we'll just go with you. I don't want to stay back here with a dead body," Roberta said.

"I agree, I would feel better staying with you," Linda said.

"All right, come along." The trio walked down the road until they came to a burned out house. Smoke still rose lazily in the air; the smell of burnt wood filled the air. A red gas can lay on its side not far from the house. "Looks like a little case of arson here," Sheriff Young said as he walked slowly up to the remains of the building.

"Why would anyone want to burn down this house? There was nothing in it." Linda said as she wrapped her arms around her body.

"You think this is it; the place you were held?" Sheriff Young asked.

"It looks like it. I don't know, I just don't know. Everything looks so different with the house gone." Linda looked around, she shivered as she looked.

"Wait a minute, there will be a fresh grave if this is the place. That is how I got away."

"What do you mean?" Sheriff Young asked.

"The fifth man was here and I think he killed one of my captors. It scared me so when the gun went off, I hid under the bed in the corner. When one of the men came to get me to take me to the bathroom, he didn't see me and for some reason he left the door unlocked. I waited for a while, and then I heard the door slam so I crawled out and tried the door. No one was in the front room only the dead body. That's when I ran. I think they may have been in back digging a grave."

"You don't say, let's have a look," Sheriff Young led the way to the back of the burned out house and stopped when he saw the freshly turned earth. "You're right, looks like a grave to me."

"Do you think that is the fifth man back there?" Roberta asked.

"It could be, but if it is why did he burn down the house. Did you leave anything behind, anything that would tell law enforcement that you had been held here?"

"No, there wasn't anything that I know of."

The sheriff took his hat off and slapped it against his leg. "It doesn't make sense. None of this makes any sense."

Chapter 18

The next morning Roberta was busy typing up a report for her father when Henry walked through the door. Roberta stopped her typing and sat in shock at the sight of him. He looked so good, his light brown hair was slicked back and his blue eyes were sparkling. If she hadn't known he had been in the hospital just a few days ago, she wouldn't have guessed it. She missed seeing him yesterday, but after the sheriff had dropped her off at the office, she had worked non-stop until closing time.

"Hi, handsome, should you be out?" Roberta asked. She couldn't stop her mouth from forming in the biggest smile in the universe.

"Hi, to you beautiful, yes, the doctor told me I could get out of the house. I'm certainly glad; I don't think I could have stood being cooped up much longer; especially with Mom hovering over me, like she did. I want to hear about yesterday. You said you would go into more detail when you saw me, so here I am."

"Well, like I told you, Mrs. Whitney showed up at the police station, looking for help," Roberta said, and then she filled Henry in on all that had happened the day before. "Then Sheriff Young dropped Mrs. Whitney off at the place where she is staying and brought me back here."

"Hump, wish I could have been with you. Instead I was stuck on the couch watching reruns and soaps. Neither of which I enjoyed."

"Oh, poor baby," Roberta laughed. "If I had only known, I could have come by and bathed your heated brow."

"Okay, okay, no more of that nonsense. I wonder why anyone would purposely burn down that old abandoned house. I sure hope the sheriff keeps you in the loop. He has all but ordered me to stay out of it."

"He did call earlier, asking Kathleen to go to the Clerk's office and see if she can find out whom that property belongs to. That is where she is now."

"I wonder who the dead man was, was there no ID at all?"

"I don't know, I'd never seen him before, but why would I. He was, maybe, in his forties or fifties, mostly grey hair, what little he had left. He had on jeans and a long sleeve plaid shirt, and the sleeves were rolled up above his elbows."

"Did he have a mole on one cheek?"

"You know, now that you mention it, I believe he did. Why? Do you know him?"

"I may. It sounds like one of the men that I see all the time out at the marina, fishing. I won't know for sure until I see him. What kind of pickup was it?"

"Hum, it was old, maybe, 1940 Chevy. It was black, I do remember that. There were several dents on it, like it had been in a scrape or two."

"It sounds so much like old man Blevins' truck, but why on earth, would he be out there?"

"Like everything else since we found Walter Whitney's body, nothing makes sense. I need to get this report finished. This is my last week and Dad is freaking out. I have promised to come in part time to do the typing, but someone else will have to keep up with the filing."

"I should be on my way; I promised Mom I wouldn't be gone long." Henry rose from his chair and walked around Roberta's desk and gave her a kiss on her cheek. "I'll call you tonight."

"I will be waiting," Roberta said with a grin.

Henry got to the door and started to open it, and stepped back as Sheriff Young pulled the door open.

"Hey, young feller, just the man I wanted to see," Sheriff Young walked in and pulled his Stetson off and laid it on Roberta's desk. "You got a minute?"

"Sure, what do you need?" Henry asked as he walked back to his chair.

"I just heard back about the ownership of that pickup we found yesterday and it belongs to a Justin Blevins. Do you happen to know him? I understand he spends a lot of time out at the lake."

"I just told Roberta that it sounded like him, when she described him."

"You mind making a positive ID on him? As far as I can tell there is no next of kin."

"No, not at all," Henry said.

"I won't have him back for a day or two; he's at the coroner's right now."

"Do you know how he died? Was it a heart attack?" Roberta asked.

"No, no heart attack, he had a couple of snake bites on his legs. Coroner said one would have got him before he could have gotten into town to a doctor, but the second one would have more than likely killed him, if not instantly, soon thereafter. Owing to where he was bit, the coroner couldn't believe he had gotten nearly to his truck. Of course we aren't for sure where he was when he was bitten. Those rattlers are one mean snake."

"Are snakes prolific out there?" Roberta asked in a low voice, her face had taken on a pasty look.

"Oh, yeah, anywhere you find shell rock like in that area; you're going to find rattlers. They love that kind of terrain, and night is a good time for them to be out."

Roberta shivered. "I'm glad I didn't see one, I hate snakes."

"Most of the time they run from you, but if you step on one, or disturb them when they are looking for food, they are one mean critter." Sheriff Young sat down and ran his hand through his hair. "I guess Miss Hamilton isn't back yet?"

"No, she said it might take a while; especially since you don't have an exact place for her to look."

"You know, you might call and tell her to see if the Blevins owned any land around there," Henry put in.

"Why are you thinking that way?" Sheriff Young asked.

"I don't know, but it makes you wonder how he knew about the place. If he was the one who kidnapped Whitney and his wife, why take them to that particular house?"

"Hum, you know, I hadn't got that far in thinking about it that way. It would make sense though if his family had owned that place he would have known that it was out where no one would ever look."

"I just spoke with the County Clerk and she's going to tell Kathleen to look for that name," Roberta said as she laid down the receiver.

"I have something else that is kinda queer, when the fire marshal was going through the ashes looking the place over, he found an old metal box. He gave it to my deputy that is keeping an eye on the place while it's an active crime scene. He brought it in when his shift ended and when I opened it, you wouldn't believe what was in it."

"Don't keep us in suspense, Sheriff," Henry said.

"It was full of money. Not just a little money, like someone's savings, I mean serious cash and some old coins that are probably worth thousands. Chief Deputy Fisk has taken it to a banker to get his estimate on the coins. I'd say if Blevins owned that place, he should have done a little looking around. No telling what will happen to it now."

"What about the grave?" Roberta asked.

"Oh, we dug it up, and it was the body of a small time hoodlum that was wanted by the Fort Worth Police. I called them and they sent a deputy over to take charge of the body, thank goodness. I have enough problems convincing the Commissioner's Court to pay for one derelict, much less the numbers that have been piling up lately. You girls must quit finding dead bodies."

Roberta laughed. "I'm sorry, it's not our fault. They just seem to pop up when we really don't want them to. I'm hoping that since I am the last of Dad's girls, this will be the end of it."

"I hope so too. It's enough to make an old man turn grey overnight," Sheriff Young said with a grin. "Oh course, I could begin to think you all are doing this to get to see more of me; me being such a handsome dude and all."

Roberta crossed her hands over her heart. "Oh, Sheriff, you found out our deadly secret, both Kathleen and I are in love with you and live for your visits."

"Now wait just a minute, Sheriff, you have stolen my girl," Henry said with a smile on his face.

"You wouldn't be pulling an old man's leg, now would you?" Sheriff Young got up and picked up his hat. "Before this gets any crazier, I'll be off. When Miss Hamilton finds out anything, be sure and let me know."

"I will," Roberta said. "Have a good day."

Sheriff Young waved his hat at her as he left the office. Henry stood up also and came back around Roberta's desk. "That gave me a chance to give my girl another kiss."

"Two in one day, be still my beating heart," Roberta said as she offered her cheek. Henry moved her chin around until she faced him and their eyes locked for a moment before he leaned down and touched her lips lightly with his.

"Henry?" Roberta said in surprise.

"We'll continue this at another time. You have work to do, remember."

"Work, oh, yes, work. I have to finish Dad's report. You'll call tonight?"

"Definitely."

Roberta watched as Henry opened the office door and turned back to blow her a kiss. Roberta grinned and blew him one back. Taking a deep breath, she turned back to her typewriter and once more got immersed in her typing.

Finishing up the report, Roberta pulled out the last sheet and began proofing it, when Kathleen breezed into the office.

"Hi, any calls?" Kathleen asked.

"No, it's been really quiet since the sheriff left. Were you able to find any information that he needed."

"Yes and no, I'll write up my report and you can type it for me. I think you are faster than I am on that thing."

That night Roberta was helping her mother with the dishes when the telephone rang. She grabbed it by the second ring. "Hello," she said breathlessly.

"Hi, beautiful, how are you doing?"

"Hi, Henry, I was beginning to worry you wouldn't call."

"Are you where you can talk?"

"Sure, why?"

"Well, after I left your office, I took a chance and went to the sheriff's office, and while I was there chatting with one of the deputy's, a phone call came in about another body being found."

"Good grief, another one? Who was this?"

"That's the thing, no one knows for sure. I managed to hitch a ride out to the site with the deputy I had been talking with. The deputy who had called it in was at the burned up house, he had spotted vultures circling. It turned out to be not far from the house;

maybe a couple of hundred yards. The body was burned pretty badly; we figure he had been in the house when it caught on fire. The thing was he had been hit over the head also, several times. That is probably what killed him."

"You have to be joking; another body and another killer. How many do we have? I can't believe this."

"Yeah, that's what we figured, but then again old Blevins could have followed him when he got out of the house and did the deed. Sheriff Young showed up with White's Funeral Home ambulance and kept shaking his head. He said it looked to him like whoever finished him off was really angry."

"Do you think the dead man could have been Phillip's dad?"

"That's what I'm thinking. The old abandoned house would have been a great temptation to him and if old man Blevins knew him, and knew he was in there that may have been the reason he set the place on fire."

"Yes, that's possible, but why would he have wanted to burn anyone alive? That is really creepy."

"I think it all goes back to that scam that Luther and Walter were running back ten years ago. We don't know who all got hurt in that scam. We know people were hurt, because Walter Whitney ended up doing time for killing one of them, but there may have been others. Blevins could have been one of them. The thing is we just don't know."

"There certainly could have been several people. I mean, a good scam requires more than one person."

"I'm going to try to find Matt Walsh today and ask him more about the scam. Luther tried to interest Matt in the scam and according to Matt, he hadn't invested in it."

"If you do, be very careful, you hear."

"I hear. Did Kathleen ever get back with any information about the ownership of that property?"

"Yes, she got back about thirty or so minutes after you left. I typed it up before I came home. It's funny you mentioning Matt Walsh, his family owned the property and according to the deed records they still own it. So what is the connection to that Mr. Blevins, do you think?"

"That is interesting, don't know if there is any connection or not, but it is interesting. Have you given the report to Sheriff Young yet?"

"No, I have it with me; I'm going to take it by there before I go on to the office."

"Let me come by and pick you up in the morning, I want to go with you and hear the sheriff's take on the report."

"It's a deal. And I want to hear what the sheriff has to say about the new dead man you all found."

"Great, I'll pick you up about a quarter to eight."

"Sounds about right, see you then."

Chapter 19

Roberta and Henry pulled up in front of the sheriff's office early the next morning. It was a cold morning with a brisk north wind blowing in to chase away the heat of the summer. There was a promise of rain in the air and Roberta shivered as she strode toward the office building.

"I could have wished the first norther of the season could have waited until a later date. I am doggone cold," Roberta said as she hurried up to the door.

Henry reached out and pulled the door open. "I agree. I guess my fishing days are all but over. I'm a fair-weather fisherman; I don't go out in the cold."

"Good morning, can I help you?" the receptionist asked.

"Is Sheriff Young in?" Roberta asked.

"I believe so; you're Roberta Hamilton aren't you?"

"Yes, I brought a report from Kathleen for him."

"I'll let him know you're here." The receptionist pushed a button and spoke on the intercom. "Sheriff Young, to the front office, Sheriff Young."

Soon the sheriff came through a door beside where Roberta and Henry were standing. "Well, well, what have we here? Can I help you?"

"Sheriff Young, Kathleen came back yesterday and had me type up the report for you on what she had found out," Roberta said as she held out the brown envelope she carried.

Sheriff Young took the envelope and opened the door to his office. "Come on in, I intended to come by your office this morning to speak with your sister personally, but seeing Henry is here with you I'll be able to kill two birds with one stone." He took off his hat and hung it on the coat rack. "Have a seat. Since you are here Roberta, you can tell me what's in the report; just a summary."

Roberta took a seat and laid her handbag on the floor. "Okay, she found that yes, the Blevins family did own it at one time, but about a little over ten years ago it was sold to the Walsh family."

The sheriff pushed back in his chair and put his finger tips together. "Really, young man, didn't you tell me that Matt Walsh and you were fishing buddies?"

"Not really a buddy, sir. Matt and I usually fished in the fishing shed at the same time. We got to talking one day when the fish weren't biting and shared a sandwich at Jacks. Other than that, I didn't really know him all that well. I do remember he and Justin Blevins acted like they didn't really know each other, in fact, Matt used to make fun of him when he wasn't around."

"Now that is interesting, of course it could have been their parents that did the land transaction not the two men."

"That's the thing; the names on the deeds were Justin Blevins and Matt Walsh," Roberta said. "The deed showed that Justin Blevins inherited the land from his mom about six months before the transaction."

"Hum, okay then, but what were their relation to Luther Johnson and Walter Whitney?" Sheriff Young asked.

"Matt told me that he and Luther grew up together and were friends. It makes sense if he and

Luther grew up together, Justin would have grown up about the same time and been friends with them also," Henry said.

"You could be right," Sheriff Young said. "It will be interesting to find out when I find Matt Walsh."

"Did you get an ID on the body from yesterday afternoon?" Henry asked.

"Oh, yes, the third dead body, it was identified as Luther Johnson. It looks like Blevins set the fire in order to kill Luther and when he saw him run out of the building followed him and finished him off. Probably got snake bit on his way back to his truck."

"That does make sense, I suppose," Henry said.

"It makes sense to me and that's all that matters," Sheriff Young said. "Oh, by the way, you remember telling me about a Lana Jacobs?"

"Yes, sir, I do. What about her?" Henry asked.

"Fort Worth police chief called me this morning early and told me they had picked her up for soliciting."

"Soliciting, really?" Roberta asked in surprise.

Sheriff Young laughed. "Not that kind, she was picked up trying to hire a hit man to kill her boss and her manager."

"Good grief, do you think that was why she was looking for Luther Johnson?" Henry looked over at Roberta and then back at the sheriff.

"According to the chief, that was exactly why she came here. It seems her step-brother was Walter Whitney's cell mate and he knew both Walter and Luther. He had told her that Walter would not do what she needed done, but that Luther just might. They have both brother and sister in jail, her for soliciting and the brother on drug charges and furnishing the contact for her in Fort Worth that might do the deed."

"How did the police get wind of what was going on?" Roberta asked.

"Fort Worth police were running a sting operation on a backroom gambling organization, and Kenny Wright, the brother, had been given a name by one of his drug dealers, it turned out that the name Kenny was given was one of the under-cover policeman on the sting operation."

They all looked at each other and then burst out laughing. "Oh, boy, I'll bet that was a shock to Miss High-N-Mighty," Henry said.

"Why do you call her that?" Roberta asked.

"That is what Matt called her, or words to that effect. What in the world did she offer the undercover cop? What is the going price for killing not one but two men?"

"That's the really funny part; she offered the policeman twenty bucks a head."

"She didn't think much of them or she wasn't serious," Roberta said in astonishment.

"The chief said that the policeman was downright offended. He said she should have been arrested for being a cheapskate. He figured anybody was worth at least a couple of hundred." Sheriff Young was still chuckling. "The chief said she screamed entrapment and demanded a lawyer. Oh well, enough laughter for the day. I should get back to deciding if Blevins was my killer or not."

"Don't you think he was?" Henry asked in astonishment. "I mean he was at the scene and there is nothing to tell us that there were two of them."

"The coroner has placed Blevins death at around nine pm; so it will depend on when he places the other death. It will have to be before nine or we have another killer." Sheriff Young stood up and shook Henry's hand. Turning to Roberta, he smiled. "Thank you for bringing the report to me. I surely appreciate it. You two stay out of trouble now, you hear."

"Thank you for your time this morning, Sheriff," Roberta said as she picked up her purse and rose. "We know you didn't have to tell us any of this, and I know I speak for Henry in saying that we appreciate it."

"Don't you be spreading any of this around," Sheriff Young said gruffly.

"No, sir, we certainly won't." Henry moved his chair back and headed toward the door. "By the way, have you notified Luther Johnson's son of his death?"

"I've got to find him; I figured he could break the news to his mom and sister."

"He works on one of the Summers Construction sites. That's where I found him."

"Thanks, I'll be able to find him then. Again, thanks for your help."

That afternoon, Roberta was putting the cover on her typewriter, when Henry walked in. She couldn't take her eyes off of him as he walked leisurely toward her. He had changed his polo shirt for a button down, plaid shirt. His aftershave beat him into the room, so he must have shaved again before he had come to pick her up.

"Hi, handsome, don't I know you from somewhere?"

"Hi, yourself, beautiful, I believe we have met before. You want to get a burger and fries at the Queen?"

"That's the best offer I've had all day. Will a milkshake go with that burger and fries?"

"Anything you ask, I will even lay my cloak down for you to walk over."

"I don't see any cloak, not even a coat. Has it warmed up out there?"

"A little, the wind has calmed down, but the temperature is dropping so your coat will feel good. Are you ready?"

"Yep, just closing down, Kathleen and Dad have left already, but I waited for you so I finished my typing."

"Sorry I'm late; I had a last minute call from Phillip. He wants to talk with me. I thought we would do that first and grab the burger when he left."

"That works for me. I wonder what he wants."

"No telling, he sounded pretty upset. I'm sure even if you didn't know your dad well, the fact that he is now dead, has to get to you."

"I'm sure it would. Where are we meeting him?"

"At Dairy Queen, I couldn't think of any other place and he didn't balk at meeting there."

"So, I can get my milkshake when we get there to tide me over."

"If the princess wishes, you know your wish is my command." Henry did a waist bow and furled his hand out to the side.

Roberta giggled as she watched him. He was so much fun. She rose and gave a short curtsey. "Then what are we waiting for?"

They hadn't been at the Dairy Queen long when Phillip walked in. He looked around and when he spotted them he walked over and sat down.

"Thanks for meeting me," Phillip said in a low voice. "I wasn't sure you would after your knock on the head."

"Hey, anything for the cause, what's up? I'm sorry about your dad." Henry said as he shook Phillip's hand.

"Mom tells me that it would have happened sooner or later. Actually, she told me that he had come to the café and she had loaned him some money. He told her that he had cancer and that was one reason he came back to Weatherford. He wanted to see her, me and sis before he died."

"Oh, Phillip, I'm so sorry. That is such an awful decease. What kind was it?" Roberta reached out and squeezed his hand.

"Lung."

"He was a smoker wasn't he?" Henry asked.

"Yeah, Mom said a pretty heavy one. He got the word before he left prison. He never said a word when I saw him. He did cough and couldn't seem to get his breath once or twice. I thought it was just from sleeping rough. I never thought about it being serious."

"Hey, man, it wasn't your fault. I understand from the news, that cigarette's will do that to you. I know a man at church that has what is called emphysema. I don't think it is as bad as cancer, but nearly."

"Anyway, that isn't why I called to have this meeting. I wanted to apologize for not telling you everything when you asked me about Dad."

"That's not a problem, he was your dad and you wanted to protect him. I understand."

"I went back to where we met on Labor Day to see why he hadn't shown up for work. I got him a job with Summers Construction. I was pretty angry with him. Of course I didn't know he was sick. I should have seen the signs, but my anger blinded me. Mom said she could tell he was sick because his skin tone wasn't good, and she said there was something about his eyes, she couldn't put her finger on it, but she knew he wasn't well. So when he told her she wasn't surprised. Back to when I went to see him, I thought he was drunk, and he may have been, that may have been his way of coping, I don't know. Anyway, I ended up calling him everything but a white man; I was so angry. I feel like a heel now. The one thing he did say was for me to watch out and protect Mom and Tammy. I asked him why and he said to be careful if Walter Whitney showed up or a man by the name of Kenny Wright. I asked him who they were and he started one of his coughing fits and never answered me. Now I'm worried, I know Walter Whitney is dead, but who is this Kenny Wright and why would he want to harm Tammy or Mom?"

"I think Kenny Wright was in prison with Whitney and your dad," Henry said. "I have a theory; you understand this is just a theory, that Whitney may have wanted revenge for being sent to prison. He may have blamed your dad for the falling apart of his scam. If Whitney did feel that way, there is no telling what he might have done."

"I can tell you this, Phillip, I spent some time with Whitney's wife and she told me that he had her find out where Wright and your dad went when they got out of prison. I guess they got out a day or two before he did. She said that Kenny was Whitney's cell mate. She knew all three because she had been on the prison ministry of her church. They were all in the services. She said it really scared her when Walter insisted on coming to the Fort Worth/Dallas area," Roberta said.

"It does sound like Whitney may have bore a grudge. I wish we knew more about that scam they ran," Henry said. "We're getting a burger here, you want one?"

"No, thank you anyway, I need to get home. Mom has taken a few days off to take care of the funeral and everything."

"Can we come to your house and talk with your mom about the time before your dad went to prison?"

"Do you think it would help, I mean, Sheriff Young seems satisfied that Mr. Blevins killed him and then died himself."

"I guess that could be the way it happened, but it doesn't feel right to me. Something's missing. I can't put my finger on it but it doesn't all fit."

"Henry and I have talked about it and we both agree that there is something missing. We won't stay long and I want to see if there is any way our church can help y'all."

"Sure, when you get through eating, come on out to the house. I'll fill Mom in on what we talked about, so she'll know where you're coming from."

"Thanks, Phillip, we'll be out there in about an hour, how is that," Henry said as the two men stood up. Henry watched as Phillip walked slowly with bowed head out of the café. He turned and smiled at Roberta, "now about that burger and fries, and didn't I hear something about a milkshake."

"You sure did. Make mine a strawberry one."

"Will do," Henry said as he walked to the counter.

After they had eaten, Henry and Roberta got in Henry's car and drove out to Phillip's home. It was getting dark when they drove up and all the lights appeared to be on in the small house.

"Okay, here we go," Henry said as he got out of the car and walked around to Roberta's side. He opened the door and watched with appreciation as she slid out of her seat. She stood up and smiled up at him. Henry smiled back as he waited for her to step out of the way so he could close the door. They walked hand in hand up to the front door and Henry knocked.

Phillip opened the door and stood in the doorway. "I'm sorry, Henry, but an old friend of Mom's has come by and I can't seem to get rid of him."

"You want me to try?" Henry asked.

"Matt Walsh isn't one to go away when you want him to. He keeps going on and on about what good friends he and Dad were, but…"

"But? Do you not believe him?"

"Not really, it seems false some way, but Mom is eating it up."

"I know Matt; maybe if I come in he will take the hint and leave."

"You're welcome to try," Phillip said as he moved to the side of the doorway to let them in.

They followed Phillip into the living room. "Mom, Tammy, this is Henry Miller and his friend Roberta Hamilton. I think you know Matt Walsh."

"Yes, I do, hello Matt, any fish biting?"

"Nope, not a bite, what are you doing here?'

"Just came by to give my condolences, how about you?"

"Same, same, I think I told you, me and Luther were old buddies."

"You mentioned it."

"Ah, Henry won't you and Roberta have a seat. I appreciate Phillip's friends coming by," Sophia Johnson said indicating the sofa.

"Thank you, Mrs. Johnson," Roberta said, "I hope we aren't intruding."

"Not at all, I have some iced tea and cake that someone brought by, can I fix you something?"

"No ma'am, we just ate, thank you anyway," Henry said as he settled on the couch.

Roberta had settled next to Tammy and she turned to her taking her hand. "I'm so sorry for your lose."

"I really never knew him, so it's hard to be sad, you know," Tammy said almost in a whisper.

"But he was your father, so there must be a little feeling of loss there."

"I guess, but not much. I just hate it for Mom and Phil. Phil especially. He feels responsible."

"Why, would he feel that way?"

"He feels like he should have insisted that our dad come here and at least sleep here."

"But wouldn't your mother have objected, they were divorced, right?'

"Yeah, but I think Mom would have let him if she had known how badly off he was."

"You mean the cancer?"

"Ah-huh."

Roberta watched tears trickle down Tammy's cheeks, and she reached over and gave Tammy a hug.

"Why would anyone want to kill him?" Tammy cried and she buried her head in Roberta's shoulder.

Sophia got up and headed toward Tammy's huddled form. "Tammy, dearest, what's wrong?"

"It's okay Mrs. Johnson, she is just crying a little," Roberta said.

"I don't know why any of you are sad about Luther. He was no good. I tried to tell you that before you married him, but you wouldn't listen," Matt said with a snarl. "Why did you have to go and marry him?"

"Matt, not now, okay, I don't want to hear this right now. My husband is dead, someone murdered him for no reason, no reason at all. He was dying, do you hear that, he was dying. He didn't have but maybe a month or two at the most. So you can just take your feelings for him and go. Do you understand, I want you to leave," Sophia stormed.

Matt pushed up from his chair, and stood staring at her as if she had suddenly grown two heads. "You still care for that no good so and so, don't you? You never gave a flip for me, even if I had worked my fingers to the bone for you."

"I loved Luther, don't you get it, I loved him, I couldn't live with him, but I loved him. I still do even though he's dead." Sophia's body shook with her sobs.

"I don't get it. I was going to get a divorce for you, I figured once Luther was dead you would turn to me. That's why I'm here. I wanted to see you alone, not with these kids of Luther's hanging around your neck. I wanted to tell you how I feel. That scumbag is dead and you and me can get married and be happy now."

Sophia lifted her head in shock. "What are you saying? Marry you, really, you have to be joking, I wouldn't marry you if you were the last man alive. Matt Walsh, you are a bigger bum than Luther ever thought of being."

"Mr. Walsh, Mother wants you to leave, so I think it is time for you to get out of here. Let me escort you to the front door," Phillip said as he took hold of Matt's arm to help him on his way.

Matt jerked his arm out of Phillip's hand and pushed himself away. "Take your hands off me, you son of a bastard." Matt headed toward the front door leaving everyone in the living room staring after him. Matt stopped just short of the front door and turned around; he had a revolver clutched in his hand. "So I'm a bum, am I? You don't understand, Sophie, you never understood, Luther was the bum not me. If I had had you by my side, instead of that whore I married, I would have gone places; I can still make it big if you marry me. The problem is all of these kids here. I'll have to get rid of them like I got rid of Luther, then you and I can go places. I may not even worry about a divorce; I'll just get rid of her too. So you move over to the side so I won't accidently hit you while I kill everyone else."

"Matt, you don't want to do this," Henry said. Henry started to stand up, but stopped when Matt cocked the gun.

"Just sit still, Henry, I didn't want to have to hurt you, but you should have told me where Luther was instead you kept stalling; saying you didn't know where he was. Of course you knew. Everyone knew, but me that is. If Blevins hadn't called me from the gas station and told me what he was going to do and why, I never would have found him. Now you and that nosey Hamilton girl will pay the price; so you just stay where you are, all of you stay where you are. Move, Sophie, move, come over here by me, you and me are going to get out of here."

"Matt, stop and think, one murder is one thing but if you murder all of us---"

Matt interrupted Henry. "One or fifteen, won't make any difference, you know what they say; it gets easier as you kill. That first one is supposed to be hard," Matt laughed. "It wasn't you know, I took great delight in killing Luther. No good double crossing scumbag, he was supposed to split the money with me after they arrested Whitney for killing that guy, but instead he made off with all of the money and then got himself arrested for theft. He was a real idiot. He had all that money and he tries to steal more." Matt shook his head.

"Matt, he didn't have any money. Whitney hid the money. Luther didn't know where. He told me all about it before he left. I begged him to forget about the money, to just get a job and we would be fine, but he wouldn't. He said he had to get a lot of money fast. That's why we fought."

Matt laughed. "You mean Whitney doubled crossed his partner, figures. I told Luther not to trust him. I helped convince Blevins to invest in the scheme, you know. Blevins trusted me, he was another fool."

"Sheriff Young, have you heard enough?" Henry asked.

Matt laughed again. "You aren't going to fool me with that old trick."

"He may not be able to fool you, but I think mine and my deputy's two guns will see your one gun and I think we'll win," Sheriff Young said and he reached around and pulled the revolver out of Matt's hand.

Later after the deputy had hauled Matt away, Henry looked at Sheriff Young and smiled. "I'm not saying I wasn't glad to see you and your deputy tonight, but how did you come to show up like you did?"

"It was just a coincidence, I had heard back from the coroner that Luther had died after Blevins did, so I knew I was looking for another killer. I got to thinking about Matt Walsh and called his house. His wife told me he had gone to the Johnson's to offer his condolences, so

I decided to take a chance and come here to speak with him. Good thing I did too."

"I'm not complaining and I don't think anyone else is."

Epilogue

Roberta, with Henry's arm securely around her, watched Patricia Ann and Stanley drive away from the church. It had been a beautiful wedding. Thank goodness she and all of her siblings were here to be involved in the wedding. They all had their close calls with death, and had come out uninjured. She looked over at her parents and saw her mom wipe her eyes with a tissue. She and her sisters had all cried a little over the last two days. Change always brought tears.

Henry squeezed her a little to let her know he understood. He seemed always to understand what she thought and what she felt. Glancing down at her engagement ring, Roberta looked up at Henry and smiled through her tears.

"Don't worry they'll be happy, just like we'll be when we marry," Henry said quietly.

"I know, but tears are part of change," Roberta said as she wiped her eyes one last time.

Looking at her family, Roberta saw the changes. Darlene was sporting an engagement ring from Jeremy, and Kathleen had told her that she thought Travis was getting her a ring for Christmas. Soon all of the Hamilton girls would be married and Roberta's mom and dad would be alone. Roberta shivered thinking about it.

"Cold?" Henry asked.

"No, oh, may be a little, the wind is sharp. I have been thinking how things are changing," Roberta said seriously.

"That's life," Henry said.

"Speaking of change, do I have to go back to college in January?"

"I promised your dad, so yes, you have to go back. We can wait; we have our whole life ahead of us. I feel like life is changing and one of those changes, as I see it, will affect the women of this world."

Roberta took a deep breath, "I guess you're right. You know I'd like to be able to stay at home like Mom and take care of the house and you, but I'm not sure I would be happy doing that."

"All of us have had our carefree time, you especially," Henry said as he grinned down at her.

Roberta wrinkled her nose at him. "I like to laugh and have fun, if that's what you mean." She stood quietly for a moment. "This year has certainly helped me grow up."

Roberta urged Henry to follow the rest of the Hamilton's back into the warmth of the church and the cleaning up that was needed.

Henry was correct the world was changing, and as 1958 grew to a close no one could see the change just over the horizon. The winds of war in Vietnam, the hippy movement, integration and the feminist movement were just a few of the changes that would come to the Hamilton family. Roberta's happy days were truly over and life was just beginning.

THE END

MAKE AN AUTHOR HAPPY TODAY!

Hey, everybody, I hope you enjoyed "Death On Labor Day". If you did, I hope you will tell others that you know about it. Please consider posting a review. Even if it's only a few sentences, it would be a huge help. This is the fourth and last in a series of what I call my 1958 series. If you haven't read the first three, you may want to get "Death on County Line", "When Death Comes Calling" and "Death Knows no Bounds."

If you think I have finished with 1958 you're wrong. I will have a new novel coming out in the near future set in the same time period and in the same town. As many of you know those were Happy Days.

Thank you so much for your help.

Clarica Burns, author

Here is an excerpt from "Death Knows no Bounds"

DEATH KNOWS NO BOUNDS

Kathleen Hamilton, eldest daughter of Robert and Sarah Beth Hamilton, sat at her desk at Hamilton Investigations, busily typing up a report that her father needed that afternoon. Sometimes she would stop and make a note on a pad of paper. Her sister, just younger than she, planned to get married at Christmas and even though nothing could make her happier Kathleen hated that Patricia would beat her to the altar. Patricia had asked her to help with the organization of the wedding and she couldn't help thinking about the various things she needed to do. Chewing on her pencil, Kathleen stopped for a minute and smiled to herself. She wanted so badly to become a private detective, but she hadn't gotten enough nerve to talk with her dad about her ambition.

Kathleen took a deep breath and went back to her typing. Wishful thinking of the future would get her nowhere; she should stick to something closer at hand like talking her dad into buying one of those electric typewriters. She smiled at the thought as she pushed the return lever on the old manual. She had gone to the high school and looked over the one they had for the students to test out. Kathleen had asked the teacher if she could try it out and got a resounding 'no'. Maybe someday everyone would be using an electric typewriter.

Her hope to convince her dad to allow her to become an investigator would probably never happen, but she could dream. In her dreams, she had become a full fledged partner in her dad's firm. It became obvious to her at age twenty-seven almost twenty-eight that she would never marry, so it made sense that she find a more meaningful career than that of secretary. Kathleen had mentioned the matter to him a time or two, but he didn't appear to take her seriously. Robert wanted her to be satisfied just being his secretary. She knew he only wanted to protect her, but she could take care of herself.

Kathleen pulled the report out of the typewriter and frowned as she proofed it before adding it to the small stack on her desk. Just as she got ready to lay it aside the outer door opened. Kathleen looked up and watched as a young man, with a blonde crew cut, turned and made sure the door closed completely.

He turned back toward the room and their eyes connected. Talk about a good looking guy, he had the bluest eyes she had ever seen hidden behind a pair of black framed glasses. His smile was tentative and a little shy. He even had a clef in his chin. Shades of Kirk

Douglas, she thought. She swallowed to keep from swooning; after all he looked close to her own age. You don't swoon over people your own age. She wondered where he had been all her life. He nervously pushed his dark framed glasses up and cleared his throat.

"I-I need to talk with someone," he stammered.

"All right, I'm someone, won't you have a seat? What can I do for you?" Kathleen asked. She gave him her best 'I'm to be trusted' smile.

"Is-is Mr. Hamilton in? I assume there is a Mr. Hamilton," he said. He pushed his glasses back up and swallowed hard.

"Do you have an appointment?"

"No, do I have to have one? I thought, you know, I thought…" He held out his hand in supplication.

Kathleen renewed her smile to reassure her visitor. "Mr. Hamilton prefers people to make an appointment. I could probably work you in tomorrow—say about five? He appears to have a full schedule until then, your name please?"

"He doesn't have anything sooner?"

"How much sooner do you want it?" Kathleen watched in fascination as he pushed his glasses up again and cleared his throat. He seemed very nervous; it made her want to soothe him and promise that everything would be all right.

"I was hoping right now. You don't know how long it has taken me to get enough nerve to even come in here. I circled the block twice before I parked, and then I sat for what seemed like hours before I had enough nerve to come up here."

"We don't bite," Kathleen said with a smile on her face.

He gave a short laugh. "I didn't think you did, but… Oh, hell, you wouldn't understand."

'I think I do, you've been watching too much television."

He gave another chuckle. "Maybe, you know all those hard nose detectives and their, 'just the facts'."

"Why don't you have a seat," Kathy indicated the wooden chair across from her desk. "I think just the facts is Dragnet and those men are policemen."

The man looked at the chair as though he had never seen one before and moved in almost slow motion to it. He looked back up at her, "yeah, but they're detectives too."

"I won't argue with you about that, let me get some information from you," Kathleen said as she pulled a steno pad out of her desk drawer.

"You-you want my name?" He stopped for a moment and grinned. "Oh course you will have to have my name. I'm sorry I'm not thinking straight this morning." He sat down and crossed his legs. Kathleen could see his nervousness by the way his foot twitched up and down.

"My name is Travis-Travis Honeycutt." He paused and looked around the office. "We are alone aren't we?"

"Of course, we're alone. Mr. Hamilton is at a meeting. It's just the two of us in the office."

"When is he coming back? Could I just wait?"

"I don't look for him back until after lunch sometime. Besides all that, he has a full afternoon."

"Oh," Travis nervously pushed his glasses back up and his foot continued to twitch.

"Mr. Honeycutt, why don't you tell me exactly what your problem is and how we may help you?"

"It's confidential," Travis said shortly.

"I'm sure it is confidential, most of our business is. We pride ourselves on being the soul of discretion. There is just the two of us in the office and I work very closely with Mr. Hamilton on all of his cases."

"Oh, in that case…" Travis looked around nervously again. "And you're sure we're alone?"

"I'm sure."

Travis swallowed hard and uncrossed and re-crossed his legs.

"Well, it's like this, I think someone may be/is going to accuse me of embezzlement."

"Oh, really," Kathleen made a note on her pad. She looked back up at him waiting for him to continue.

"What did you just put down?" Travis asked trying to peer at her writing.

Made in the USA
Columbia, SC
07 May 2021